DEC. 7

D0446894

EMMA
DARCY

man in the park

Harlequin Books

TORONTO • NEW YORK • LONDON
AMSTERDAM • PARIS • SYDNEY • HAMBURG
STOCKHOLM • ATHENS • TOKYO • MILAN

Harlequin Presents first editon August 1986
ISBN 0-373-10903-2

Original hardcover edition published in 1986
by Mills & Boon Limited

CHAPTER ONE

THE door behind her opened. Susan resisted the impulse to glance around. She really needed this job. She kept her gaze fixed on Miss Ainsley, hoping the woman was favourably impressed by her. So far there had seemed no flicker of interest in the measuring grey eyes and Susan had no inkling of how well or badly the interview was going. It surprised her when the marble-smooth face suddenly broke into welcoming life.

'What can I do for you, James?'

'The Cargill File. Is the update complete?' It was a warm honey voice, a voice which tempted any listener to turn its way.

Before she could stop it, Susan's head had turned. Curiosity was instantly replaced by goggle-eyed wonder. Never in her life had she seen such a stunning-looking man. Not in the flesh. He was sheer dream-factory material, the kind of man one sees in a top-line fashion magazine or on a movie-screen.

'Yes, it's finished. Sorry I didn't bring it in to you. I've been busy with these interviews.'

Interview! The word caught back Susan's attention. She tore her fascinated eyes from the man and looked anxiously at Miss Ainsley, horribly aware of an embarrassed flush creeping up her neck. How hopelessly gauche of her to stare so obviously! Fortunately the woman was riffling through some manila folders on her desk, apparently oblivious to Susan's reaction.

'Ah, here it is.' The grey eyes held a

5

caressing softness as Miss Ainsley picked up the folder, inviting the man to come forward and take it.

'Interviews?' The voice asked with ear-tingling interest.

Then he was walking past Susan's chair, taking the folder, turning. Vivid blue eyes raked Susan from head to foot, then twinkled their amusement at her. He had caught her stare. The flush raced into Susan's cheeks and felt like a fiery furnace under her skin.

'Christine is leaving,' Miss Ainsley stated in a dry, bored tone, no longer inviting interest.

'Well, thank God for that small mercy! Her voice always grated on my ear.' He propped himself against the desk in an indolent pose which suggested he was in no hurry to leave. 'And who is this young lady?'

Susan felt like a butterfly on a pin. It was all she could do not to squirm in her seat under the gaze of those fantastic eyes. The face was unbelievably handsome in a strong, very masculine mould, the features clear-cut, chiselled from a distinctive bone-structure which would always be striking, even into old age. The toffee-coloured hair with its blond streaks was casually styled and the darker brown of his eyebrows was the perfect contrast to a golden-tan skin which seemed impossibly smooth for a man. The three-piece light grey suit, white shirt and pale blue tie clothed a tall, athletic body in tailored perfection.

'A Miss Hardy,' came the reluctant introduction.

'Speak to me, Miss Hardy.'

Susan did not know what to say. Hopelessly tongue-tied she looked to Miss Ainsley for direction.

The woman's mouth curled and there was a glint of dry mockery in the grey eyes as she came to the rescue. 'This is Mr James Kelleher, our leading barrister in chambers.'

'How ... how do you do, Mr Kelleher,' Susan stammered.

His teeth tugged at the full lower lip for a moment and then he smiled a dazzling white smile. 'I do quite well thank you, Miss Hardy. What was your last job?'

'I ... I was the receptionist in a solicitor's office. I handled all the telephone calls in and out.'

'How old are you?'

'Twenty-one.'

'And you're not about to run off and get married?'

'Married? Oh no! I don't even know anyone,' she denied in flustered confusion.

'Miss Hardy has just arrived from the country,' Miss Ainsley supplied sardonically.

The tone was a giveaway. Susan knew now that Miss Ainsley was not impressed. She could kiss this job goodbye. Disappointment dragged at her heart. Another failure to add to a growing list of failures.

'Hire her.'

Astonishment, then relief and joy lit Susan's face as she turned gratefully to the man. He had said it. He was smiling. He really had said those words.

'James, I do have other girls to interview.'

The waspish reproof dimmed Susan's joy. She darted an anxious look at Miss Ainsley. The grey eyes were sharp with annoyance. Susan glanced back at the man, hoping against hope that his direction would prevail. The good humour had vanished and a cold arrogance hardened his face as he turned to the woman behind the desk.

'Erica, you will hire Miss Hardy.' Warm honey had changed to icy steel. 'She would not be on the short-list of applicants for interview if her qualifications and references were not satisfactory.' His gaze swept back to Susan, giving her a look of such warm appreciation that her heart curled. 'Miss Hardy not only has a pleasant voice, she is also very pleasing to the eye, which will be a remarkably pleasant change from the last two additions to our staff.'

'Those girls are very efficient workers,' Miss Ainsley retorted indignantly. Two spots of angry colour suddenly highlighted her cheekbones.

James Kelleher flicked her a mocking look and his voice dropped to a soft purr. 'A woman doesn't have to be plain to be efficient, as you very well know, my dear Erica.' His smile held a suggestion of smug triumph. 'I shall look forward to seeing Miss Hardy behind the front desk. She will add an attraction which has been singularly lacking in our reception area. Good morning, ladies.'

With an elegant sweep of the head which encompassed both of them he pushed away from the desk and strode from the room. Susan's nerves prickled with the tension he had left behind him. Erica Ainsley's heavily mascaraed lashes veiled her eyes, but the thinning of her lips suggested clenched teeth and the pen which had been rolling between fingers and thumb suddenly spun on to the desk. Susan held her tongue for fear of saying the wrong thing.

The woman was some years older than Susan, good-looking in a cool, austere way, her long neck accentuated by upswept blonde hair which had been coiled around her crown. The careful make-up, pearl studs in her ear lobes, the powder-blue suit; all presented a career-woman image which had made Susan feel very unpolished. At last she moved, leaning back in her chair and looking down her long, patrician nose at the girl sitting opposite her. Susan felt reduced to insect-size.

'Well, Miss Hardy, you have the job,' she stated coldly. 'I hope you can live up to Mr Kelleher's expectations behind the front desk. I wouldn't advise you to harbour any other expectations. Mr Kelleher senior does not approve of fraternisation between the professional and supporting staff.'

Good Lord! I'm being warned off, Susan thought incredulously. But on the heels of that thought came the marvellous realisation that she definitely had been given the job. Her smile was pure delight. 'Oh, thank you, Miss Ainsley. I promise you I'll be very efficient.'

Even Erica Ainsley's stiff prejudice came unhinged in the face of such natural exuberance. She smiled, although the smile was tinged with irony. 'You don't have me to thank, Miss Hardy. However, you may fit in quite well. We'll see, won't we? Be here at nine o'clock, Friday morning. Christine will explain the switchboard to you before she leaves.'

The note of dismissal was quite distinct. Susan rose to her feet, dark eyes sparkling with happy relief. 'Nine o'clock, Friday,' she repeated eagerly.

One delicately plucked eyebrow arched higher.

'Might I suggest that you come in a more appropriate style of dress? As Mr Kelleher pointed out, you will be on show in our reception area and while your ... uh ... present outfit might have been suitable for the office of a country solicitor, something a trifle more subdued is required here.'

'Yes. Yes, of course,' Susan gabbled, blushing furiously at the criticism and mortified at having been found wanting in her choice of dress. 'I'll go shopping now,' she added unnecessarily.

'Do that, Miss Hardy,' came the smug little rejoinder.

It made Susan wonder if Erica Ainsley was simply being bitchy but the suspicion was quickly rejected. The floral cotton skirt and matching sheer blouse did seem out of place here. Nevertheless, the older woman had enjoyed pointing out a shortcoming in taste and Susan's delight had been effectively dimmed.

'Good morning, Miss Ainsley, and thank you again,' she said self-consciously.

A cool nod was her only answer.

Susan let herself out of the office. Her squashed spirits quickly lifted again as she walked into the reception area. It was a far cry from the shabby bench seats, threadbare carpet and the battered tin ashtray which were all that had greeted Mr Everingham's clients back home.

Here was quiet luxury. The cinnamon fleck in the thick, beige carpet had been picked up in studded, leather armchairs. Lustrous, indoor plants gave a restful contrast of colour with their variegated leaves. Handily positioned coffee tables offered onyx ashtrays and a selection of glossy magazines. On the walls hung an amusing collection of black and white sketches, caricature drawings of Leo McKern in his role of 'Rumpole of the Bailey'. Despite her nervousness Susan had smiled over them while waiting for her interview.

Now she smiled with pleasure at the thought of working in these surroundings. The receptionist's desk was situated behind a high bench which effectively hid the switchboard and any clutter of paperwork from waiting clients. The girl behind it threw Susan a furtive look as if not wanting to catch her eye. She had an over-long face. A neat fringe disguised the high forehead and the short, brown hair had been fluffed out to give width. It was the deep chin which spoilt what was really a pleasant face. On impulse Susan stepped over to the bench.

'Excuse me. Are you Christine?'

Light blue eyes expressed surprise. 'No, I'm not. Christine has just gone out for a moment. Can I help you?'

'I ... I just wanted to say hello. I'm starting work here on Friday morning,' Susan explained a little self-consciously.

The long face became longer as the jaw dropped in open amazement. 'You got the job?' Recovery was swift. 'Please forgive me for being so rude but I didn't think you had a hope when you came in. I'm Denise, by the way, Denise Rowe. I didn't mean that I thought you'd be no good or anything like that. It's just that ... well, you're not the type of girl Miss Ainsley would normally hire.'

Susan flushed. 'Actually it was Mr Kelleher who said I was to have the job.'

Eyebrows disappeared under the fringe. 'The gorgeous James?'

Susan nodded.

'Oh boy!' It was almost a whistle of glee followed by a grin of anticipatory relish. 'This ought to be interesting. I'm really looking forward to having you work here ... uh ...' Her eyes dropped to the appointment book. '... Susan is it?'

'Yes. Susan Hardy.'

The grin grew wider. 'Good for you, Susan. That sure is one in the eye for ...' A telephone buzz demanded her attention and she turned aside with a cheery wave. 'See you Friday.'

Susan returned the wave but before leaving she noted the elegant style of Denise's slimline dress. The cream bouclé knit was banded around neckline and sleeves with a soft gold which was repeated in a tie-belt. Her own wardrobe certainly needed updating, she decided, as she walked out into the corridor which led to the elevators.

When the doors in front of her opened, two men stepped out and both heads turned towards her as Susan moved past them into the compartment. I can't look too terrible, she mused, catching their interested eyes as she pressed the down button. Once out on the bustling city streets, she privately assessed her reflection in shop windows.

Maybe she should have her hair cut in one of those short, sophisticated styles. But then a short style might be difficult to manage. Her long, black hair was very thick and very straight and it might stick out at all angles if cut short. Its sheer weight made it fall tidily to just below her shoulders and a slide-comb above one ear kept it away from her face. No, her hair would have to do as it was.

It had always seemed odd to Susan that her eyelashes and eyebrows were not equally straight. The thick, curly fringe of lashes made any further accentuation of her dark eyes absolutely superfluous. Her eyebrows rose in a satisfactory arch but their outer wings curled upwards and only the most assiduous plucking forced the arch downwards again.

As for the rest of her face, Susan had no real complaint. Sometimes she wished it was more oval and less round. Her small, slightly upturned nose occasionally caught too much sun. She was blessed with a clear, creamy skin and a natural blush of colour in her cheeks. Too much revealing colour at times for Susan's liking. Try as she might to be coolly poised, her cheeks invariably betrayed any rush of emotion. Her mouth was a satisfactory shape and she had good, even, white teeth.

Her figure was not as fashionably slim as it probably should be but Susan was above average height, tall enough to carry generous curves. As for her clothes ... she eyed her reflection critically. No one could say the floral skirt and blouse were loud or objectionable. The soft tones of pink, aqua and lemon were pretty and feminine. In fact the outfit was one of her favourites.

James Kelleher had not seemed to notice anything wrong with her clothes. He had thought she was pleasant to look at. 'The gorgeous James.' Susan sighed. They didn't breed men like him back home, that was for sure. City-sleek and heart-catchingly handsome. And that's what she had to become. City-sleek. Like Erica Ainsley and Denise Rowe. It was simply wasting time to be mooning along when there was a mission to be accom-

plished. With a firm sense of purpose Susan began
casing the shop windows for the right kind of
clothes.

The display of summer fashions was positively
dazzling. And confusing. Some of the way-out
styles with their glitter and wild colour combina-
tions seemed far too improbable for actual
wearing. Susan found herself continually drawn
into looking at the feminine clothes she had always
fancied. A black-and-white gingham dress which
featured flounces of broderie anglaise held her
gaze captivated for a long time and only the
most rigid discipline forced her to pass it by.
Unfortunately, the dresses which seemed to hold
the essence of class also held daunting price-
tags.

After some hours of dithering indecision and
with feet protesting at the tight constriction
of court shoes, Susan gave up the idea of
buying anything and caught a bus home. Only
the prospect of ruining her tights prevented
her from discarding her shoes altogether on
the two blocks' walk from the bus stop to her
sister's house. Normally it was a pleasant walk.
Lane Cove was a pretty suburb and the front
gardens along Julia's street were all well-
established and beautifully kept, a credit to
their owners. However, they did not receive
their due admiration from Susan today. Each
step was wincing agony for her cramped toes.
It was absolute heaven to close Julia's front
door behind her, kick her feet free of shoes
and sink her suffering toes into the softness of
carpet.

'Is that you, Suz?' came the stage whisper from
the kitchen.

'Yes. Coming through,' Susan replied in an

equally hushed voice. It was a relief to know that the children had not yet awakened from their afternoon nap. She could talk to her sister without interruption.

Julia pounced on her as soon as the kitchen door was safely shut. 'How did it go? Do you think you have a chance?'

Susan grinned triumphantly. 'More than a chance. I got the job.'

'For sure?' Julia squeaked, then gave her younger sister a gleeful hug. 'Oh, Suz! That's marvellous! I told you you could do it.'

'Not me. It was Mr Kelleher who did it. I'd never have got the job without his say-so. Let me sit down and I'll tell you all about it. My feet are killing me. I don't think I'm ever going to get used to wearing high heels all the time.'

'You will,' Julia assured her.

Susan grimaced. 'I'll have to. Miss Erica Ainsley would have a fit if I wore my old sandals. As it is, you're going to have to help me shop for clothes, Julia. It seems that what I'm wearing won't do and I've been walking around the city in circles trying to find something suitable, all to no avail.'

'Who's Erica Ainsley? And Mr Kelleher?'

Under her sister's deft cross-examination Susan related every detail of the morning's interview. Julia's satisfaction became increasingly smug as James Kelleher's intervention was described.

'You've caught his eye. And no wonder. You don't realise how stunningly pretty you are, Suz.'

'Oh, come off it, Julia. You should see him.'

'He's interested. Definitely interested,' came the

voice of authority.

Susan smiled. 'Well, according to Miss Ainsley he's not allowed to be, so don't start dreaming for me, Julia.'

'You can't take any notice of that green-eyed bitch.'

'Grey-eyed.'

'She fancies him for herself and doesn't want competition. Spite and jealousy,' Julia tossed off airily. 'Never you mind, love. I'll steer you to some clothes that'll knock his eyes out.'

'I don't think that's supposed to be the object of the exercise,' Susan commented drily.

'You can kill two birds with one stone. We'll go shopping tomorrow while my cleaning lady is here to mind the kids.'

The back door was suddenly banged open and two noisy schoolboys came clattering into the kitchen with breezy greetings and demands for something to eat. Susan watched Julia handle her eight-year-old and six-year-old sons with the efficiency of long practice, asking questions about their day's activities while providing them with drinks, fruit and biscuits. Julia was the super-organised housewife and mother, and at thirty she was still as pretty as she had been when Brian had married her.

She was smaller and slimmer than Susan and her face was more angular, but she had the same dark eyes and thick black hair, worn short and cleverly layered to shape around her head. Susan admired her sister who always seemed so sure of herself and what she wanted out of life. Julia didn't float. She was a ball of dynamic energy. She organised her husband with shameless bossiness but Brian seemed quite content to let her do so. As a dental surgeon he led an organised professional life so it probably suited him to have his social life organised for him.

It was a happy household and Susan was very grateful to Julia for pushing her into coming here and for all the help she had offered and given. Susan realised now that she had been floating, achieving nothing, going nowhere. Much as she missed her parents and the small-town pace of Lamamby, Sydney was the place to be if she was to break free of the past and start a new life.

The door into the hallway was pushed open and Derek, Julia's four-year-old, came trailing in with Lindy in tow. Being one year older than the little girl, he had adopted the role of boss and protector ever since Susan and Lindy had arrived. As always, Susan's heart caught at the sight of her beautiful little daughter and her arms flew out to gather her in as Lindy ran across to her.

'Hello, darling. Been a good girl for Aunty?'

Lindy nodded and Susan lifted her on to her lap to cradle her close.

'Derek woke me up but I had enough sleep. Can we go to the park now, Mummy?'

'In a little while. After we have a snack and change our clothes.' Susan stood up, still hugging Lindy to her. She waited until Julia's boys stopped chattering for one moment, then said quickly, 'We'll go on down to the flat now, Julia. Thanks for everything. I'll see you in the morning.'

'Nine-thirty. We'll get an early start.'

'Sure you can spare the time?'

'It'll be my pleasure to get you spruced up for the kill.'

Susan laughed at the relish in her sister's voice.

She did not imagine that James Kelleher had found her as attractive as Julia made out, but there was an excited tingle in her blood at the thought of seeing him again.

The granny flat was spacious enough to cater for all Susan's and Lindy's needs. It was a self-contained unit which had been built on to the back of the house for Brian's mother, who had lived in it for several years before unexpectedly departing to marry an elderly widower. The large living-room had a kitchenette at one end with a breakfast bar divider. The one bedroom easily housed two single beds. A combination bathroom-laundry led off the bedroom. The furnishings were all in autumn tones which were easy to live with. Both Susan and Lindy had been delighted to set up their own little home here.

Lindy's dolls adorned the bedroom. Plastic toys sat around the bath. Susan had hung pictures in the living-room, filled the shelves with framed photographs, ornaments and books, and dressed up the lounge suite with the cushions she had embroidered with satin appliqués. A television set, radio and cassette-player provided home entertainment and Susan found a pleasant freedom in being independent of her parents for the first time in her life.

Having set Lindy at the breakfast bar with a glass of milk and a peanut-butter sandwich, Susan downed a glass of milk herself then changed into jeans and T-shirt. She strapped comfortable old sandals on to her poorly used feet, thinking that every change in life carried necessary adjustments, but wishing that dressing up in style did not require high heels.

Lindy bounced in to the bedroom, demanding

to be dressed in similar clothes and chattering non-stop about a game she and Derek had played. Since having Julia's boys as playmates Lindy had lost much of her shyness, although she was still wary of Brian. She was not used to a father-figure, which made it rather odd that she had taken so readily to the man in the park.

Dave. Dave Brown. And his scruffy dog, Wally. No scruffier really than Dave himself. Dog and owner suited each other. At first Susan had been wary of the man who seemed to have taken up occupation rights to the bench near the swings. Every afternoon he was there, slouched on the seat, legs stretched out, the dog crouched at his feet. He invariably wore cotton-drill, baggy trousers which were paint-stained, and unironed cotton shirts, their long sleeves untidily rolled up above his elbows. While he did not quite have the air of a derelict of the human race, he had certainly looked somewhat unsavoury with his unkempt curly beard and his riotously curly, long brown hair.

Susan had tried to keep Lindy away from the dog but it had proved an impossible task. Although a bigger animal, it had a similar appearance to the Australian silky terrier owned by Susan's mother, and Lindy had gravitated to it with relentless frequency. Wally was a friendly, lolloping beast who begged for attention and finally Dave had spoken up.

'Wally loves kids. Why not let your little girl play with him? They'll both enjoy it.'

For the first time Susan had looked him straight in the eye and had been surprised to find friendly hazel eyes twinkling up at her.

'I'm harmless, too,' he had added with a reassuring grin.

It had been a totally disarming grin and Susan had found herself smiling back, despite the man's scruffiness. He had introduced himself and invited Susan to sit down next to him. After only a small hesitation she had done so. She still knew very little about him but she enjoyed their idle conversations in the park.

Dave had a dry sense of humour and an enormous store of general knowledge. He was well past thirty and she often wondered why such an intelligent man had apparently given up on life. Occasionally, she had glimpsed a deep well of sadness in his eyes, but he kept their conversations impersonal and Susan did not attempt to breach his privacy. She accepted him simply as the man in the park, a person with whom she could talk on all manner of subjects.

It was obvious that he genuinely liked children. He did not talk down to Lindy as many adults do with awkward condescension. He listened to her childish prattle with warm interest and answered all her questions good-humouredly. Susan felt at ease with him too, which was strange because he was so different from anyone she had ever met.

She supposed the city threw up people like him, worldly-wise, careless of what others thought of him, deeply cynical about what life was all about. Still, he was an interesting person and it was pleasant to talk with someone outside the family. And Lindy loved playing with Wally. Dave had informed them that the dog was half-labrador, half-silky terrier, an improbable cross-breeding which nevertheless explained its appearance and affectionate nature.

Susan finished brushing Lindy's hair and tied it

into two bunches with fresh ribbons. Mother and daughter were startlingly alike. Lindy had inherited little from her father, only the slightly pointed, pixie-like ears. The rest of her features were a mirror-image of Susan's, even to the eyebrows which kicked up instead of down. The dark, almost black eyes shone with excitement as they set off for the park.

It was only three blocks away, but on the other side of the main road into the city. Susan had to hold Lindy's hand firmly as they waited for a green light at the pedestrain crossing. When the 'walk' sign finally blinked on, Lindy almost dragged Susan's arm off in her eagerness to reach the other side.

'Wally! Wally!' she called impatiently, even before they had entered the park gates.

Its floppy ears flattened back as it ran, the dog came tearing across the grass. When it seemed that he would jump up and knock Lindy over, Wally pulled up short and rolled over on his back for a tummy tickle.

'You ridiculous animal!' Susan laughed as Lindy knelt down to oblige.

Wally ignored the insult. He rolled his eyes back in ecstasy. Only when Lindy stopped tickling did he spring back on to his feet. Very gently he leaned his front paws on Lindy's chest and licked her chin.

'Come on, Wally. Let's build a big castle,' Lindy suggested, then ran off towards the sandpit, the dog bounding excitedly at her heels.

Dave was occupying his usual seat, slumped in his habitual pose, indolently watching the world go by. His elbows were hooked on to the back-rest, outstretched legs crossed at the ankles, beard sunk on to his chest. He was a tall man and, although his forearms were quite muscular, he was altogether too thin for his frame. He obviously needed looking after since he didn't seem to care enough to look after himself. Sometimes Susan itched to tear his shirt off and take it home to iron.

'Hello,' she smiled.

One hand lifted in acknowledgement of the greeting. 'You're looking pleased with yourself today,' he remarked drily. 'Win a prize in the lottery?'

Susan's smile widened into a grin. 'Better than that. After a month of answering advertisements, I've finally got a job.' She sat down and looked at him for congratulatory comment.

Dave frowned deep lines of disapproval. 'Why do you want a job? Who's going to look after Lindy if you go out to work?'

The unexpected criticism rankled. 'Some people go to work to make a decent living,' she replied tartly in oblique criticism of his non-productivity. 'And my sister will look after Lindy as if she was her own daughter.'

'But she's not your sister's daughter. She's yours,' came the forceful retort. Then bitterly, 'I can't abide people shunting the responsibility of their kids off on to someone else. What's wrong with your husband? Can't he support you? Or is it that you want more than he can provide?' The sharpness dropped to a sour grumble. 'That's the trouble these days. Everyone grasping for goodies and losing their humanity. You shouldn't damned well have kids if you're not prepared to look after them.'

'And just what the hell do you know about it?' Susan demanded hotly, jumping to her feet as angry indignation chased away the initial shock of his outburst. 'It so happens that I don't have a husband to support me and while you might be able to exist on the dole, Dave Brown, I want Lindy to have more than what's possible on an unmarried mother's pension. And she won't lack for love either, so mind your own damned business!'

Tears burnt her eyes as she turned on her heel and strode towards the sandpit. He had spoilt all the pleasure in her success. And soured the casual friendliness of their relationship.

'Susan . . .'

A hand caught her shoulder and gripped hard, halting her in her headlong flight to gather up Lindy and go home. She rounded on her tormentor, trembling with heightened emotion. Brilliant black eyes stabbed him with hurt and contempt.

'What right do you have to judge me, Dave Brown?'

'None. None at all,' he said softly.

The apology in his voice and the deep compassion in his eyes were Susan's undoing. The unshed tears started trickling down her fiery cheeks and her mouth quivered as words choked on the lump in her throat. She had never had to explain her position before, never had to account for Lindy's existence outside the respectable bonds of marriage. Everyone back home had known and accepted what had happened. Susan had been given sympathy and kindness, never criticism.

The tears fell faster and still she was wordless. Suddenly the city seemed an alien, cruel place. She should never have come here. She had been safe in Lamamby, cocooned in an unchanging little world which she had understood, and which had understood her.

Then to her startled amazement Dave stepped forward and enclosed her in a strong embrace, gently pressing her head on to his shoulder and stroking her hair in soft comfort. Even more amazing was her lack of inclination to resist what he was doing. She had never been in any man's arms but Kev's, yet it felt good to lean on Dave at this moment. He exuded a warm caring which seeped into her soul and soothed the jumble of fears.

'Forgive me,' he murmured, and she felt his deep sigh. 'You inadvertently opened some old wounds and I lashed out at you without thinking. I'm sorry, Susan. I had no right to assume anything, but a girl like you ... it seems incomprehensible that Lindy's father would not have wanted to marry you.'

A wave of old grief brought a sob to her throat. 'He did. He did want to marry me.'

The hand stroking her hair stopped. 'Didn't you want to marry him?' was asked softly.

'Oh, yes. It was all we wanted. Ever since we were fourteen.' And the words spilled out of a deep well of desolation. 'We'd waited so long. Our parents made us. They said we were too young. But it was too long. Kev died ... killed in a road accident ... just a week before our wedding. I was ... I was two months' pregnant.'

'Oh, Christ! You poor kid!'

And she cried. Cried as she had not done in a long time. Cried for the life she and Kev had planned. The life they would never have together. Cried for the boy, the man she had loved with all her heart. The father Lindy would never know. And Dave held her safe until all the tears were spent.

CHAPTER TWO

TIME had stopped. Life had stopped. There was only a vacuum of remembrance, a greyness of soul which devoured all other existence. Slowly, tiredly, Susan opened her eyes. They gazed blankly at formal gardens; zinnias and marigolds bordered by petunias and phlox; groves of trees in the background. Swings. Slide. See-saw.

'Lindy!' she gasped, horrified that she had forgotten her daughter even for a moment. She pushed away from the man holding her, frantic to reassure herself that Lindy was all right and hoping that the little girl had not witnessed her mother's distress.

Dave soothed her anxiety. 'It's all right. I've been watching her. She's still in the sandpit with Wally. Hasn't even glanced our way.'

'Oh! I . . . thank you. I . . . I didn't mean . . .' she stammered in a flood of embarrassment. It was so awful, shaming to have broken down like a weak idiot, weeping on to the shoulder of a man in a public park for anyone to see.

'Nothing to be ashamed of,' Dave said quietly. Then as she hurriedly glanced around, he added, 'And no one took any notice. They don't in the city, you know. It's called "not getting involved".'

'Oh!' she said again, rather stupidly. Back home it would be the talk of the town if she had behaved in such an openly uncontrolled manner.

'Come and sit down again. Relax.'

He took her elbow and steered her to the bench. Susan sat stiffly, still feeling hopelessly self-conscious. Dave flopped down into his loose-limbed slouch.

'Why did you come to Sydney?' he asked curiously.

'My ... my sister lives here.'

'I mean why leave home? You're a country girl through and through.'

'Why do you say that?'

'Susan ...'

He sighed and she darted a glance at him. His mouth was curling into an ironic smile. He caught her glance and held it, his eyes soft with a knowledge which was as old as time.

'There's no artifice in you. You're an innocent. If you stay in Sydney you'll have to grow a hard, protective shell or the city will gobble you up, change you, corrupt that innocence. It has no time for open-hearted people. The rat race specialises in looking out for number one and the winners don't care about the losers.' He hesitated, then asked, 'Were you unhappy at home?'

'No. No, I wasn't unhappy. But ... it was as Julia said ... there was no future there for me and Lindy. You see, I'd always been Kev's girl ... Kevin Logan ... my ... my ...'

'The man you were to marry,' Dave supplied helpfully.

Susan nodded and sucked in a steadying breath. 'There was never anyone else. Never would be. Lamamby is a small town, more or less revolving around the sawmill and the logging industry. Most of the young people move away unless they're involved in family businesses or properties. Kev's father was the town accountant and Kev was going to follow in his footsteps. I learnt to type and worked for the local solicitor. After ... after I had Lindy, I went back to work part-time for Mr

Everingham. If I'd stayed in Lamamby, that would have been my life. Julia said . . .'

'That's your sister.'

'Yes. She's nine years older than me. She came to Sydney when she left school, wanting to become a nurse. She married Brian who's a dental surgeon. They have three sons.'

'And what did Julia say?' Dave prompted, apparently not particularly interested in Julia's life.

'They came to visit at Christmas time and Julia said I was crazy letting my life drift by. She said I was too young to live on memories, that it was time I broke free and did something positive. She pointed out that . . . that Kev needn't be the only man for me. Only in Lamamby. And Lamamby was a dead hole in which I was needlessly burying myself and depriving Lindy of . . . of ever having a father and a normal family life.'

She turned anxious eyes to Dave, wanting his approval. 'Don't you think she was right?'

He seemed to consider the question for a very long time. His gaze drifted away from hers, brooding on an inner world to which Susan had no entry. 'I guess there comes a time when one should let the past go. Start again. If there's a reason for starting again. And you're young . . .' the hazel eyes swept back to her with a wry sadness, '. . . very young. Yes, your sister was right, Susan.'

He sighed and slouched even further down on the seat, dropping his head on to the back-rest. 'At least it was quick and clean . . . your tragedy. And he left you a beautiful daughter to remember him by. Someone to love. You've got a purpose in life, a reason for picking yourself up and moving on. There are some who are left with nothing. A couple I knew ... a pair of struggling artists ... they had a daughter.'

The pause was so long that Susan was tempted to prompt him into continuing, but the grim set of his mouth did not invite prompting. She sensed that what he had begun to say was very close to him, possibly too close to give away in a casual confidence. Struggling artists. She glanced down at his paint-stained trousers and wondered if he was speaking of himself.

His mouth suddenly twisted out of its tightness. 'The whole irony of the situation was that the man didn't want a child. The couple weren't married. Didn't want to marry. The woman simply fancied having a baby. She let herself get pregnant and announced the fact afterwards.'

'Did they marry then?' Susan asked quietly.

His grimace was very sour. 'No marriage. Jeannette was a bird of freedom. She didn't want any ties. Why she ever imagined she wanted a child is beyond me. But the child was born. A beautiful little girl. Melanie. She was an absolute delight from the moment she entered this God-forsaken world. The years passed. Jeannette's work began to catch the art critics' eyes and was selling well. The father of the child was doing all right with commercial work. Melanie started school. But she didn't cope very well. Always seemed listless, over-tired. The doctors diagnosed leukaemia.'

'Oh no!' The horrified gasp was out before Susan could muffle it.

Dave did not seem to hear. He continued his story as if driven to get it out, expelling the poison from a dark, festering place. 'There was test after test. One hospital after another ... all no use except to verify that there was nothing they could

do to save her life. Jeannette couldn't cope with it.
Or didn't want to. She walked out. Selfish,
irresponsible bitch!

'It took Melanie three years to die and she only
had her father to cling on to. She used to cry for
her mother at first but she grew resigned. Even
grew resigned to her own death, though her father
never did. Eight years old. A brave little wraith of
a child. She died holding her father's hand.'

Susan's eyes brimmed with tears. The poignant
sadness of the little girl's death and Dave's lonely
suffering tore at her heart. There was no doubt in
her mind that the father was Dave. It explained so
much about him. He was a man who had been
drained of any purpose or joy in life. The
harrowing experience of having to stand helplessly
by and watch one's daughter gradually sink
towards death would make anyone feel a dreadful
futility in everything.

And there had been no one to share the burden
of grief and inner torment, no one to alleviate the
pain and sense of frustration. Susan understood
now why he had so bitterly criticised her about
leaving Lindy for Julia to mind. He had been
thinking of Jeannette. But it was not a similar
situation at all. Susan would never turn her back
on her daughter, not for anything.

She wanted to reach out to Dave, offer him
compassion, but his air of withdrawal rejected any
such impulse. In any case, he had made a
sympathetic gesture impossible by distancing
himself from the events described, speaking of the
father as another person altogether. Perhaps that
was the only way he could cope with the
memories.

Susan, on the other hand, had only good
memories of Kev. The tragedy of his death had

been the killing of a promising future, for him, for Susan and for Lindy. But Susan's grief was not flavoured with bitterness and her family, indeed everyone in Lamamby, had been supportive in the aftermath of the accident. She had not been alone as Dave had been alone . . . was still alone. Except for his dog. Melanie's dog? Was that why Wally had attached himself to Lindy so readily?

'Sorry for going morbid on you,' Dave said abruptly and hitched himself forward as if shrugging off his cloak of depression. He sent her a wry little smile. 'Don't suppose I made you feel better at all.'

'Yes, you did,' Susan replied quickly. 'You made me see how well off I am and how much I should be grateful for.'

His eyebrows lifted in surprise. 'Did I? I must be wiser than I thought I was,' he added self-mockingly.

'Dave . . .' She wanted to tell him that he was not so old that he couldn't start a new life, too, but she suddenly realised how presumptuous that would be. 'Where do you live?' she substituted, conscious that he was waiting for her to speak.

'Not far from here,' he answered vaguely. 'What about you? Are you living with your sister's family?'

'Yes and no. There's a flat attached to the back of the house. I'm quite independent really.'

'That's good,' he nodded. 'Your sister sounds as if she could be a pretty dominating lady. You don't want to let her run your life entirely, Susan.'

'I can dig my heels in when I want to,' she assured him.

'Are you expected at the dinner table this evening?'

'I get our meals in our own kitchen. Lindy's and

mine, that is. I wouldn't want to intrude on Julia and Brian.'

He nodded, hesitated, then said, 'I was just thinking. Perhaps you and Lindy might like to join Wally and me in a meal at McDonald's instead of going straight home from the park.'

The loneliness in his voice pierced her soul and it was on the tip of her tongue to accept the invitation when she remembered that she had no money. The park was free. She had not bothered to bring her handbag.

'I'm sorry, Dave. I can't. But it was kind of you to ask us. Another time perhaps.'

'Sure.' He sighed and bent forward, resting his elbows on his knees, shoulders hunched over, head hanging low. 'Just thought Lindy might enjoy it. Mel ...' He swallowed the name and added sharply, 'Kids usually love the French fries and thickshakes.'

Her heart went out to him, but what could she do? 'It's just that I haven't any money with me,' she explained regretfully.

He turned his head, wary eyes searching out sincerity. 'If you'd like to go, it'd be my pleasure to buy you and Lindy a meal.'

'Can you afford it?' She flushed in embarrassment at the bluntness of her question. 'I mean ... well, I can pay you back tomorrow. I couldn't accept your ... your generosity. That wouldn't be fair.'

His face relaxed into a smile. 'I can afford it.'

'I wouldn't want you to go short because of us,' she said worriedly.

His smile widened into an amused grin. 'I promise you I won't go short.'

'Then we'd be very happy to come with you,' she declared, relieved that the matter had been resolved. She hoped their company would help Dave put aside the painful memories she had unwittingly stirred.

Lindy came running up in infantile high dudgeon. 'That boy over there . . .' She pointed accusingly. 'He kicked over my sandcastle. I told Wally to bite him but he only barked.'

The dog looked up adoringly and wagged his tail, completely unaware that he had failed to do his duty.

'If Wally started biting people a policeman would come and take him away,' Dave explained gently. 'You wouldn't want that, would you, Lindy?'

Her eyes rounded in alarm. 'Oh no! I love Wally.' Immediately she squatted down and gave the dog a hug which was close to a stranglehold. Wally slurped an appreciative tongue up her cheek.

Susan leaned forward and tucked some stray hair behind her daughter's ear. 'Never mind the castle, love. Would you like me to give you a swing?'

'A high one,' Lindy demanded eagerly.

She was off and running before Susan had even moved. 'When do you want to go and eat?' she asked Dave as she rose to her feet.

He waved a careless hand. 'Whenever. I've all the time in the world. Let Lindy play as long as she likes.'

It was almost six o'clock when they finally set off for McDonald's. Dave had produced a leash for Wally from his pocket and Lindy insisted on holding it. Wally did not really need to be restrained. He trotted along beside them, only stopping occasionally to sniff a gate or a telegraph pole.

They were in no hurry. The February evenings were long and balmy, the heat of the day still lingering on the air. The extra hour of daylight saving meant that darkness did not fall until well past eight o'clock. Their companionable silence was only broken by Lindy's bossy instructions to the dog. The street they walked along was tree-lined and a light breeze rustled the leaves. Flower scents wafted from freshly watered gardens.

It was a very pleasant stroll and Susan was grateful that Julia and Brian lived here in Lane Cove. The inner suburbs of Sydney were a concrete jungle; tall, narrow little houses crammed together without a garden in sight. The thought of living in such close confinement made Susan shudder.

Several tables were set on a small lawn outside the McDonald's cafeteria. Dave tethered Wally to a stool, invited Susan and Lindy to sit down and took their orders. He came back with what seemed a terribly overloaded tray. Even when he had served Susan and Lindy with their orders, three huge hamburgers and two large bags of French fries remained for him.

Susan shook her head in amazement. 'Can you really eat all that?'

'No.' He grinned. 'But Wally will devour anything.'

And to Susan's further amazement he tore two bags open and set hamburger and French fries down on the grass for the dog. Wally wolfed into the food as if he had been waiting for it all day.

'Honestly, Dave! That's sinfully extravagant,' Susan scolded. 'He would have been just as happy with a can of dog meat.'

'Now, there you're wrong. Wally thinks he's human. He always eats the same as me. Won't touch canned pet food. And I don't blame him. I won't either. Smells awful.' He wrinkled his nose at her but his eyes were twinkling mischief.

Susan sighed. 'You're crazy. No wonder you have no money left for anything but essentials.'

'I have all the money I need. If your wants are small you don't need much,' he reasoned matter-of-factly.

. 'But, Dave! If you were more careful you could . . . well, at least get yourself a haircut and some decent clothes.'

He raised a mocking eyebrow. 'Does my appearance offend you?'

She frowned at his levity. 'You must know you look a mess. Why don't you at least iron your shirts?'

'Can't be bothered.'

'Then why buy cotton? Why not get nylon shirts that don't need ironing?'

'Hate nylon next to my skin. It makes me itch.'

She rolled her eyes in exasperation and because he seemed to have a ready answer for everything she fell back on munching her hamburger.

His eyes teased her. 'Maybe, sweet Susan, I prefer to be liked for myself, not for finely pressed tailoring or a barber's skill.'

'Huh!' she threw at him derisively. 'The truth is, Dave Brown, you've fallen into a sloppy rut and you're too lazy to get yourself out of it.'

He chuckled, a deep throaty sound which was pleasant on the ear. 'You could be right.'

Maybe he needed to be scolded, needed to be shown that someone cared about him and what he was doing to himself. Susan herself had been guilty of floating along. Julia had goaded her out of the easy path of passivity. Perhaps she could do the same for Dave.

'You'd feel better if you trimmed that beard and got a haircut,' she said coaxingly.

He stroked his beard and raised his eyebrows in disdain. 'I'll have you know, young woman, that even Sir Walter Raleigh in his prime did not have such lustrous locks as these. To cut them would be pure sacrilege.'

She had to laugh at his outrageous claim. Dave grinned at her, his eyes alight with devilment. At least she had cheered him up, Susan thought with satisfaction, even though he had turned aside her suggestions. He burbled on about the fickleness of fashions and how ridiculous it was to place any importance on them.

Susan's thoughts drifted to the morning's interview and Erica Ainsley's emphasis on correct dressing. Dave was right. It did seem stupid. Yet necessary if she was to fit into the job for which she had been hired. A picture of James Kelleher flashed vividly across her mind. The clothes had been part of the man, completing the perfect image. She wondered how Dave would look in such clothes and decided that his beard and long hair would make nonsense of them.

'I can't eat any more, Mummy. I'm full,' Lindy declared, handing over a half-emptied bag of French fries.

'That's okay, Lindy. Want your thickshake now?' Susan inserted a drinking straw through the punched hole in the lid and passed the carton to her daughter.

'I don't think I can drink all this.'

'You can give what's left over to Wally,' Dave assured her. 'He loves chocolate thickshakes.'

Lindy spoke down to the dog. 'I'll leave you a real lot, Wally.' And in fact she drank very little before sliding off her stool.' She removed the drinking straw and the cardboard lid, knelt down next to Wally and carefully tipped the carton so he could easily drink out of it.

Susan finished off the left-over French fries and started on her own thickshake, enjoying the creamy coldness on her tongue.

Lindy started to giggle. 'Look at Wally. He's got his head stuck in the carton.

The dog was indeed a comic sight, wriggling on his back with forepaws attempting to drag the carton off. He finally succeeded and then attacked the carton as if it was an enemy to be shredded to pieces. Dave bent over and gathered up the resulting debris while Susan collected the litter from the table. Their meal was over and it was time to be setting off for home.

The stroll began in high spirits but as they approached the park Lindy complained that her legs were too tired to walk any farther. Much to the little girl's delight, Dave offered a piggy-back ride and Susan was handed Wally's leash.

'Your beard tickles my arms,' Lindy giggled as she was hoisted into position.

'Think of me as a horse and you're hanging on to the mane,' Dave advised.

'Giddy-up, horsie!'

Dave obligingly broke into a trot, Wally barked and pranced around excitedly, and by the time they reached the pedestrian crossing they were all breathless from laughter.

'That's enough, Dave,' Susan protested. 'It's another three blocks to Julia's house. It's been a lovely outing and I don't want to take you out of your way. I can manage Lindy from here.'

Her protest was promptly overruled by both Dave and Lindy. They continued as before, Dave giving forth a stream of nonsense which had Lindy giggling all the way. At Julia's front gate he lifted her down with an exaggerated swing which brought a squeal of delight. Susan smiled her gratitude at his kindness.

'Thanks, Dave. It was very good of you to take us out and bring us home.'

'Thank you for giving me the pleasure of your company. I can't remember when I last enjoyed an evening so much.' He took Wally's leash and smiled down at Lindy. 'Be a good girl for your mother now.'

'I'm always good,' Lindy declared smugly.

He laughed and turned away. Wally gave a little whine of regret then fell into step beside his master. Scruffy dog. Scruffy man. But both with hearts of gold, Susan mused as she took Lindy's hand and walked down the side path which gave private entrance to the flat.

The back door to the house opened and Julia poked her head out. 'Susan, come up and join Brian and me in a cup of coffee. Lindy can sit with the boys in the T.V. room.'

Susan? Julia rarely used the full name. Something was wrong. 'All right,' she nodded and lifted Lindy up the steps.

The boys welcomed their little cousin and soon had her quietly settled. Julia whisked Susan off to the dining-room and pointedly shut the door. Brian looked up from his evening newspaper. He was very much the clean-cut professional type; neat brown hair, gold-rimmed spectacles, strong nose, firm mouth and chin.

'Ah, Susan,' he began in his slightly heavy manner. 'Congratulations on getting the job. Good position. A very reputable legal family, the Kellehers.'

'Never mind that now, Brian,' Julia snapped,

almost pushing Susan into a chair with one hand while snatching up the percolator and pouring coffee with the other. She attacked with barely a breath taken. 'Who was that hairy hippie I saw you with at the front gate? Here you are, late home from the park and when you finally turn up, it's with a disreputable looking character who should probably be run in on a vagrancy charge.'

'Dave's all right, Julia. I know he looks untidy but ...'

'Dave! My God! Haven't you any sense? You've obviously told him your name. You show him where you live. This isn't the country, you know.'

'Julia's right, Susan.' Brian's calm voice was appreciably lower than his wife's shrill tone. 'You have to be careful in the city. People can be very plausible and you can be taken for a ride. A very unpleasant ride. You'd be well advised to mix only with those to whom you've been properly introduced. Now maybe there's been no harm done, but where did you meet this man?'

'In the park.'

'In the park!' groaned Julia.

Susan turned on her impatiently. 'There's nothing bad about Dave, Julia. I've been talking to him for weeks. He's a good, kind man and Lindy likes him too. I know he looks scruffy but he's an artist who's a bit down-and-out at the moment.'

'An artist!' Julia scoffed. 'Anyone can call themselves an artist. What's he doing in the park?'

'Exercising his dog,' Susan retorted irritably, although it was not quite true. Wally exercised himself. Dave just sat.

'Susan ...' Brian cleared his throat. 'You must understand that we feel responsible for you and Lindy, particularly while you're still new to the city. We want to safeguard you against getting involved with the wrong kind of people. Of which there are many. For all you know, this ... artist ...' he curled his mouth around the word as if it was distasteful, '... could be into drugs. His appearance certainly suggests the possibility. People on drugs don't care for themselves.'

'Dave's not on drugs,' Susan declared with utter certainty.

'How do you know?' Brian persisted.

'I just know. Look!' Her hands lifted in appeal. 'He lost his daughter recently. She died of leukaemia and he's ...'

'Then he's married,' Julia jumped in.

'No. The woman he was living with walked out on him when ...'

'There you are!' Julia crowed triumphantly. 'That shows the type of man he is! And what on earth you think ...'

'Julia, that's enough!' Susan snapped with such uncharacteristic sharpness that her sister was left open-mouthed. 'Now you listen to me,' she continued, her hackles well and truly up. 'That man nursed his daughter through three years of illness. When she died he fell apart, didn't care about anything any more. I happen to know that feeling and he has my deepest sympathy. This afternoon he was depressed and lonely and he invited us to go to McDonald's with him. He just wanted company. That's all. So we went and had a very pleasant meal and he walked us home. You might think I'm terribly wet behind the ears, and I probably am as far as city-life is concerned, but I'd trust Dave with my life. With my life,' she repeated vehemently.

The ensuing silence was charged with the emotion she had poured into Dave's defence.

Perhaps the memory of Susan's grief over Kev's death softened Brian's stance, for when he spoke again it was in a kindly tone.

'Well, you'll have to forgive us if we erred on the side of caution, Susan. Julia was concerned when you were late home and your ... uh ... friend did look rather unsavoury.'

Susan sighed. 'I'm sorry, Julia. I didn't think of worrying you.'

'I'm sorry, too,' Julia muttered and drew in a deep breath before offering a peace-making smile. 'Guess I was coming the heavy older sister, but I do so want you to find someone you can be happy with, Suz. This man ... well, if you say he's a good person I suppose I'll have to accept that ... but he's not the sort for you to get involved with.'

'I'm not getting involved with him, Julia. We're simply friendly acquaintances. I find him interesting to talk to while I'm watching Lindy play. He's much older than me, you know. Well into his thirties, I'd say. He knows ... oh, something about everything. He must read an awful lot.'

'All the same, don't get into the habit of going out with him, Suz. He might become dependent on you and Lindy for company and start seeing Lindy as a substitute for the daughter he lost. It's one thing to feel sorry for a person, quite another to become his emotional crutch. You've had your own grief. Don't take on someone else's when you should be looking for some future happiness.'

Susan knew her sister meant well. What she said was very sensible but it didn't apply to Dave. He was too proud a man to accept sympathy or allow anyone to help him. He did not want to be helped. However, it was too difficult to explain the complexities of Dave Brown's character to someone who had never met him. It was easier to let the matter drop.

'I can see your point,' she said tactfully.

'Perhaps it would be wise to ... uh ... taper off your meetings with him,' Brian suggested ponderously.

'If I think that's necessary, I will.' Susan would concede no more than that. She was not going to deprive Lindy of playing in the park and she had no intention of snubbing Dave.

'Anyway, you won't have time to be going to the park so much once you start work,' Julia said with satisfaction.

'That's right,' Brian agreed with even more satisfaction. 'I must say you've done very well for yourself getting this job, Susan. You'll be meeting the right class of people there.'

'Not to mention James Kelleher who's right on the spot,' Julia put in archly.

'He probably won't take any notice of me once I'm part of the furniture,' Susan said drily, covering her irritation at Brian's emphasis on class. He also probably meant well but she bridled against the innate snobbery of his attitude.

'My dear Susan,' he said indulgently, 'no one, and I mean no one, would ever see you as part of the furniture. Their eyes will undoubtedly be on you.'

The heavy-handed compliment brought a self-conscious blush to her cheeks.

'Particularly when we get you into some smart clothes,' Julia added smugly. 'We'll have a marvellous day shopping tomorrow.'

'Yes, well, thanks for the coffee, Julia.' Susan rose from the table. 'I'd better get Lindy down to a bath. I'll see you in the morning. Good night, Brian.'

'Good night, my dear.'

Susan lay awake for a long time that night, over-tired from a day which had put her through a gamut of emotions. Her mind would not relax and blank out. She wondered how much circumstances shaped people into what they were. She had no doubt that James Kelleher had been born with a silver spoon in his mouth. He looked as if he had always been polished to brilliance. Erica Ainsley? What frustrations and hopes had driven her into the mould of career woman? Brian, she imagined, had never stepped outside the conventional pattern and nothing had ever ruffled the smooth tenor of his life.

It was strange to think that Brian and Dave were much the same age. Her brother-in-law had a closed, self-satisfied mind, everything sorted into neat, tidy compartments of right and wrong. Dave, on the other hand, had an open, roving mind which attacked any subject from a variety of angles, forcing Susan to think of other points of view besides the ones she had taken for granted. He provoked, he teased, he led her into new paths of thought and she regretted that their meetings would be curtailed when she began work. Still, there were always weekends.

And it would be good to be working again. The totally new environment would be an interesting and exciting challenge. Perhaps the 'gorgeous James' might take an interest in her. Who knew what the future held? Susan suddenly realised that it had started already. She was no longer drifting nor even looking back. She was thinking ahead.

CHAPTER THREE

IT had been a terrible, terrible day. She had arrived at the office feeling smartly dressed in her new red and white outfit, and Erica Ainsley's sour greeting had been, 'We are not running a barber's shop, Miss Hardy. Do please try to fit in.' And that had only been the beginning!

The pace had been hectic all day. Demanding. Bewildering. Confusing. Nothing like the office of a country solicitor. This was a big city law practice with four busy partners—Kelleher, Kelleher, McIlroy and O'Toole—and numerous clerks and typists. Susan found herself in a pivotal role, the connection between all these people plus the clients. The switchboard was a nightmare of lines. And she had blundered. Badly. She had coped with mixed-up lines by giving effusive apologies but the *urgent call* had been a horrendous blunder.

Never interrupt a conference between lawyer and client, she had been told. Take a message. Ring through the message as soon as the conference is over. Except there were some people who were always put through immediately and Susan had rigidly denied access to one of these VIPs. Mr McIlroy had torn strips off her with a tongue so acid that Susan still burnt at the memory.

Christine had been no help at all. From the moment she had arrived she had whined about the imminent railway strike which could ruin her honeymoon. She had not been the least bit interested in teaching Susan anything, and had

44

gone off on a two-hour lunch break which had resulted in the word-processor fiasco.

Susan had never even been in contact with an office computer before today, let alone a word-processor. She was a good, accurate typist but it was not typist's skills required so much as a working knowledge of the coded commands. She had been handed a computer-disc and forms which had to be changed. In her ignorance she had typed in information which had over-written and destroyed other important data on the disc. Christine had returned from her prolonged lunch hour, discovered the damage and insisted that Susan report to Erica Ainsley and shoulder the blame. She had been subjected to another tongue-lashing, virulent with sarcasm, which spelled out the message, 'Shape up or ship out.'

Christine was given the responsibility of restoring the data to the disc and she sniped at Susan for the rest of the afternoon. Susan had to handle the switchboard alone and, in trying to keep an eye on how Christine operated the computer, she made a few more wrong connections. Eventually she felt the switchboard could be mastered with full concentration but the computer/word-processor represented a potential disaster area unless she learnt its intricacies very fast.

With this in mind she had telephoned Julia, telling her that she had to work late and asking after Lindy. That had been the crowning error of the day. Some malicious fate had brought Erica Ainsley to the front desk right at that moment and Susan had been sharply berated for making personal calls in office hours.

Only Denise had been pleasant to her, commiserating over the blunders and encouraging her to believe that Monday would not be so bad. It was to Denise she had turned at five o'clock, begging her to set up the computer safely so that the coded commands could be practised and learnt.

Now, finally, all was quiet and peaceful, except for the sick churning in Susan's stomach. Try as she might to apply the instructions in the computer manual, she could not manipulate the example on the screen in the manner described. It was hopeless. Hopeless. Monday was still looming as a minefield where wrong steps would be inevitable.

'Hello there! Susan, isn't it?'

The golden honey voice told her it was James Kelleher before she turned around. His dazzling smile made her heart skip a beat as she rose to her feet.

'Yes. Susan Hardy. Can I help you, Mr Kelleher?'

'No. Just returning documents to the office.'

'Was . . . was your case successful?' Denise had told her he was to be in court all day. He seemed to be in high spirits and her interest in him prompted the question before discretion could hold it back.

'Very successful.' His grin was pure satisfaction. 'And you? Did your first day go well?'

'I'm afraid not.' She sighed then added wistfully, 'But I hope to do better on Monday.'

'What are you doing here?' He glanced at his watch. 'It's almost six o'clock.'

'I'm trying to figure out how to use the word-processor so I won't make any more mistakes.'

Her grimace was more expressive than she knew. To her surprise he laughed.

'Believe me, Mr Kelleher, it wasn't funny,' she

said earnestly. 'If I don't get everything right on Monday, I think Miss Ainsley will fire me.'

'Such gloom!' he intoned, too amused to inject sympathy into the words. 'We can't have that happen, Susan. Not when I championed your cause. It would give Erica far too much satisfaction. Switch that machine off and come out to dinner with me. I feel like company and you can tell me your tale of woe. A good meal and a bottle of wine will dull the pain.'

The invitation was so unexpected and so unexpectedly gratifying that an acceptance leapt to her tongue. Only the sure knowledge that the computer still had her beaten made her hesitate.

'Mr Kelleher, there's nothing I would like better, and thank you very much for . . .'

'You're not going to refuse,' he declared winningly.

Her heart sank. 'I've just got to learn this or . . .'

'Take the manual home with you. Study it over the weekend. Better still, go to a computer centre tomorrow and get someone to demonstrate a word-processor to you. So much easier to grasp if you're actually shown everything,' he advised.

Relief untied all the nasty knots in Susan's stomach. 'I hadn't thought of that.'

'So you'll have dinner with me.'

'I'd love to, Mr Kelleher. Thank you very, very much.' Her smile beamed with gratitude and pleasure.

The blue eyes measured her speculatively for a moment. 'You really are a strikingly beautiful girl, Susan Hardy. I shall enjoy having you sit across from me at table.'

She blushed, then suddenly recalled Erica Ainsley's comment on her dress. 'You're very kind, Mr Kelleher. I'm afraid . . . are you sure I look all right to be taken out? Miss Ainsley said my dress was wrong,' she said in a squirming rush of uncertainty.

His mouth quirked sardonically. 'Yes, I can well imagine Erica saying that. A vibrant poppy far outshines a pale piece of porcelain. Don't let her drain you of colour, Susan. You'd gladden any man's eye, precisely as you are. And I think your dress is perfect for you,' he declared with ringing conviction. 'Get ready to go while I dispose of this briefcase.'

Susan stared at the door swinging shut after him, scarcely believing her luck and dazed with delight at the prospect of dining out with James Kelleher. Then, anxious not to keep him waiting, she plunged into a flurry of activity; switching off the machine, replacing the disc in its cover and carefully filing it back in its storage slot, placing the all-important manual with her handbag and telephoning Julia.

'You're not!' came Julia's gasp of incredulity. Then quickly, 'Stay out as long as you like. Don't worry about a thing. I'll put Lindy to bed up here. Enjoy yourself. And Suz ... don't go all shy on him.'

'Julia, he's only being kind because I've had such an awful day,' Susan insisted, playing down the excitement tingling through her own veins.

'Huh!' said Julia.

'I must rush and comb my hair. Give my love to Lindy. 'Bye now.' Susan rang off in a state of pleasurable confusion.

James Kelleher was waiting for her when she returned from the rest room, assured that she was at least tidy. Very conscious of his approving gaze she quickly tucked the manual under her arm and proclaimed herself ready. Ready for what, she wondered as he took her free hand in his and smiled down at her. He really was the most handsome man she could imagine. Only he was real. And he was taking her out.

'Where do you live?' he asked interestedly.

'Lane Cove.'

'That's handy. On my way home, too. I know a little restaurant at North Sydney. Superb French cuisine. Do you like French cooking?'

'Oh yes.' She was quite prepared to like any kind of cooking tonight even though her experience of haute cuisine was almost nil. There would surely be something on the menu she could eat.

They took a lift down to the basement car park where Susan was led to a silvery-grey BMW. The seats were covered with soft lambswool and she sank into hers with an appreciative sigh.

'Lovely car.'

'A bit conservative for my personal taste. It was a diplomatic choice.'

'Diplomatic?' It seemed an odd word.

He grinned. 'A rising young barrister cannot afford to appear racy. My father's words.'

'Oh!' Tasteful, classy, expensive. The right image. His clothes and car were certainly right but what about Susan? Did she fit into the acceptable mould? She chided herself for leaping too far ahead. As she had told Julia, this dinner date was an act of kindness. But James had said she was beautiful. And her dress was perfect. A little thrill of satisfaction brought a smile to her lips.

'Happier now?' he asked teasingly.

'Yes, thank you.'

'Well, tell me the whole catalogue of first-day horrors.'

As they drove towards the Harbour Bridge and across it, Susan recounted everything that had gone wrong for her. James was in turn, amused, sympathetic and helpful in response. By the time they pulled up in a narrow, back street of North Sydney, Susan's terrible, terrible day had somehow been reduced to a not-so-bad day, in fact a perfectly understandable day which could be comfortably shrugged away.

The restaurant was small, only six tables set in what had obviously been the front parlour of the old terraced house. The décor was dark and very Victorian, in keeping with the style of the room with its ornately plastered ceiling and picture rail around the walls. Cream lace tablecloths, little posies of fresh flowers and brass table lamps provided light touches against a wallpaper of burgundy watered silk and an equally dark red carpet. Old portraits of stiffly posed families hung on the walls and Susan wondered if they were people who had inhabited the house a few generations ago.

The hour was still early and not surprisingly they were the first patrons to arrive. A dinner-suited waiter greeted them, settled them at a table, served them with glasses of sherry and presented handwritten menus for their perusal. There were only four choices for each course and Susan's mind boggled at the list, struck by a sudden panic that there was nothing she could order with confidence. Rather than betray her ignorance she decided that the smoked salmon could not be too different in taste from ordinary tinned salmon and the chicken dish had to be basically chicken, however foreign the sauce. James ordered Avocado Bisque and the trout dish, to be accompanied by a bottle of Chardonnay which Susan soon discovered was a pleasant white wine.

With the food problem settled, Susan relaxed

and smiled at James. 'I've been doing all the talking. Tell me about your court case. Was it before a jury?'

'Yes, thank God!' He laughed at her quizzical expression. 'Juries can be swayed. Judges tend to focus on points of law and I'm afraid in this case, my client was technically guilty.'

'And you got him off?' Susan could not hide her shock.

His grin was unashamed. 'That's what I'm paid for.'

'But if you knew he was guilty . . .'

James shook his head in amusement at her naïveté. 'Susan, we're probably all guilty of breaking the law at one time or another. In this case the defendant had not really harmed anyone. He'd been juggling company money to his advantage and someone blew the whistle on him. Most of the directors of the company were aware that he was feathering his own nest but that's common practice at that level and they turned a blind eye because the man was such an able administrator in all other respects. It was to no one's advantage that he be sentenced to imprisonment, except perhaps the person who squealed on him.'

'You mean there's one law for the rich and another for the poor,' Susan said with some resentment.

'No. But the rich can pay for the best legal talent.'

'Such as you.'

His smile just escaped being smug. 'I would have to admit I do have a way with a jury.'

Susan could well imagine that. He would have a way with anyone. She sighed and gave a wry little shrug. 'Well, it still doesn't seem right somehow.'

'Probably not,' he agreed. 'But one must be realistic. The wealthy and powerful can beat the law almost every time. They either pay their way out of trouble or bring influence to bear on the case. Either way they go free, and if you think about it, it's not a bad thing. The world won't run without leaders and the very quality which makes them leaders puts them above the general public. Some concessions should be made to them in return for what they achieve for all the rest.'

'I suppose so,' Susan murmured, not at all sure that she agreed with him. Nevertheless he certainly was fascinating to listen to and look at; the lovely, rich tone of his voice, his expressive hand gestures, the attractive movement of his lips, the extraordinary blueness of his eyes.

The starters arrived and Susan was able to do justice to the smoked salmon. It made her thirsty and she sipped the wine while James finished what had proved to be a creamy soup. The empty dishes were whisked away by the attentive waiter.

'Erica mentioned you were from the country,' James commented questioningly.

'Yes. I've lived in a small town all my life. Julia, my older sister, persuaded me I should come to Sydney and try my luck here. I didn't have much luck at all until you gave me this job,' she said gratefully.

'I'm glad I was on the spot to help. A girl like you doesn't deserve to be buried in the country. What on earth have you been doing there all this time? Didn't you say you were twenty-one?'

'Yes. But it's not so bad in a country **town, you** know. It's really very pleasant.'

He skilfully drew her out about Lamamby, the kind of life its citizens led and the work she had done for Mr Everingham. She did not tell him about Kev and Lindy, not wanting to introduce so personal an element into the conversation. Their relationship was employer/employee and, until it was definitely more than that, Susan was reluctant to confide the intimate details of her life.

The chicken and trout dishes were served and Susan found the sauce really delicious with its flavouring of mushrooms and shallots. She decided that French cuisine had a lot to recommend it. Conscious that she had been talking on a subject which probably didn't interest a person like James Kelleher, she asked him what he thought Sydney had to offer its inhabitants.

He reeled off a whole catalogue of cultural activities, listed its scenic charms, then entertained her with pithy descriptions of the various amusements available.

'You'd make a marvellous tourist guide,' she declared appreciatively.

He shook his head. 'I couldn't imagine a more boring occupation. I have my own life to live and I wouldn't want to live it showing others how to live theirs.'

Susan felt a twinge of disappointment. She would have liked him to show her some of the places he had described. However, she supposed that was hoping for too much. She imagined that James Kelleher was used to more sophisticated company than hers and she would not hold his interest for long, if at all.

The restaurant was filling up by the time they had finished their coffee. Susan noticed the waiter throwing them a measuring glance as if checking to see whether they would soon leave. James seemed in no hurry to go. He requested a glass of port. Susan declined any kind of after-dinner liqueur, feeling decidedly mellow from the wine she had already consumed. Besides, it was dizzying enough to have those vivid blue eyes regard her warmly from across the table.

'What's your address in Lane Cove?'

Susan told him, thinking he wanted to know which route to take her home.

'Can you arrange private transport into the city next week?'

'I catch a bus. There's a good service not far from home.'

'But the buses will be packed out long before they reach you with this train strike on.'

'Is it definite?'

'Yes, it's been announced. No trains after midnight tonight. Can you get a lift to and from work with someone you know?'

Susan shook her head. Brian's dental surgery was in the neighbouring suburb of Chatswood and she couldn't ask Julia to drive through peak-hour traffic just when the children needed her. 'I'll have to get up extra early and hope for the best. Miss Ainsley won't be too pleased if I'm late for work,' she added with a despondent sigh.

'Precisely what I was thinking. You'd better come with me.'

'With you?'

He smiled. 'Well, I have to protect my interest in you. Erica must not be given any reason to complain of my choice.'

Interest. My choice. His lovely voice gave the words special meaning and Susan's heart curled with pleasure. Surely this was more than kindness. Her dark eyes danced with happy anticipation.

'That's very good of you, Mr Kelleher. I don't know how to thank you.'

Twinkling amusement suddenly darkened to something else. A shivery sensation crept up

Susan's spine. With a little shock she recognised the look as sexual appraisal and Susan wasn't sure if she was flattered or repelled.

'Oh, I think we could make that James out of office hours,' he drawled softly. 'Are you ready to go now?'

'Yes. Yes, thank you,' she said quickly, quelling the nervous flutter in her stomach.

She was being silly. He found her physically attractive. And she certainly found him attractive. It was only natural to translate that attraction into sexual possibilities. Only Susan was completely unprepared for it. For almost four years her sexual instinct had lain dormant. She had not even been out with a man, let alone been aroused to thoughts of lovemaking.

No, that was not quite true. She had been out with Dave but that didn't really count. Dave didn't see her as a desirable woman and she regarded him simply as a friend. James Kelleher was an entirely different proposition. And he was very much an experienced man of the world. Not like Kev. She had grown up with Kev and their progression towards lovemaking had come naturally with the process of growing up. James Kelleher was practically a stranger.

She watched him settle the bill with a credit card, noted the deferential manner of the waiter and decided that James Kelleher would not be diffident about taking what he wanted. His air of confidence was ingrained by years of success. Success in every field, she imagined.

On the way out of the restaurant he took her arm and as they walked towards the car, Susan was pricklingly aware of the lithe strength in the masculine body which brushed against hers. He saw her settled into the passenger seat. Susan tried to calm her disordered pulse rate while he rounded the car and took his place behind the driving-wheel. Instead of turning on the ignition he looked at her, a long, lingering look which held the suggestive warmth of an intimate caress.

'Now where?' he asked softly.

Fear of making a fool of herself formed the answer. 'Home please.'

One eyebrow arched questioningly. 'To Lane Cove?'

She hesitated. Did he expect some other answer? 'Yes, of course.'

His smile held a hint of mockery as he repeated, 'Of course.'

What else could she have said, Susan fretted as he started the car and turned it towards the highway. Surely it was up to him to invite her somewhere if he wanted to prolong the evening. She hoped he had not taken her words as a rejection of his interest. She simply did not know what was expected of her in this kind of situation. After all, he was her employer and this hadn't exactly been a date, had it? Confusion kept her silent on the drive home and James did not offer any further conversation.

When he turned the car into her street he directed him to Julia's house and wondered if she should hop out or wait for him to open the door. As soon as the car stopped she quickly unbuckled her seat belt and reached over to the back seat for the computer manual. By that time James was out of the car and the question was settled. Employee or not, he was offering her every courtesy. He opened her door. Susan swung her legs out and stood up. A warm rush of blood swept into her cheeks as she met his eyes.

'Thank you very much.'

'My pleasure.' The words were a deep purr. The warmth of his gaze held hers captive. His hand lifted. Fingers gently stroked her burning cheek and trailed slowly down to tilt her chin upwards.

She knew he was going to kiss her and excitement flicked through her veins. She watched his mouth come closer and her own quivered in anticipation. His lips brushed across hers, a sensual promise which was not fulfilled. He withdrew, leaving her tingling with expectancy. Again he stroked her cheek.

'Thank you for your charming company. Will eight o'clock suit you on Monday morning?'

'Yes. I'll be ready,' she got out huskily, wishing he would kiss her again. With more fervour.

He smiled. 'I shall expect you to tell me you're an expert on word-processors.'

'I'll do my best,' she promised him with an answering smile to cover her disappointment. There was not going to be another kiss.

He closed the passenger door and steered Susan to the pavement. 'Will you be all right from here?'

'Yes. Thank you again.' She looked up at him, a shy invitation in her eyes. 'Good night.'

For a moment it seemed he hesitated. Then the hand on her elbow gave a light squeeze and fell away. 'Good night, Susan.'

He gave her a jaunty wave as he drove off. Susan stared after the tail lights until the car turned a corner and swept out of view. Feeling curiously deflated, she took her time walking to Julia's front door. It was not late and she knew her sister would be waiting to pounce on her with questions about James Kelleher. Susan was not sure of the answers. His kiss had been too fleeting to tell her anything positive. Perhaps there was nothing positive to tell, and yet she had not imagined that strong projection of sexuality in the restaurant.

She shrugged away her bemusement. James's manner on Monday morning would probably clarify where she stood with him. Meanwhile she had enough to worry about, making sure that she understood the workings of a word-processor. She fished out the door key from her handbag and went in to face and fend off Julia's questions.

She hoped Lindy had not been upset by her mother's defection tonight. Susan felt a twinge of guilt. She really should have come straight home instead of dining out with James Kelleher. Dave would not have approved of her actions. It had been selfish of her to disregard Lindy's needs just because she found a man attractive. But Susan wished that James had kissed her again.

CHAPTER FOUR

DAVE was not at the park. Lindy called and called for Wally but the dog did not come. Susan hid her own disappointment and tried to make up for Lindy's by helping to construct an elaborate road system in the sandpit. The little girl was not completely consoled but at least she was distracted.

They had not visited the park since the trip to McDonald's. Lindy had come down with tonsillitis the very next morning and had not been well enough for outside play until yesterday, when Susan had started work. This morning she had been very grumpy about her mother's trip to the computer centre and only the promise of an afternoon in the park had cheered her up. But the park was not as much fun without Dave and Wally.

Susan found an old carton in the rubbish bin and fetched some water from the drinking fountain to hard pack the sand. She constructed two mountains and Lindy carefully dug tunnels through them while Susan began a bridge across the gorge in between. It was almost finished when Wally landed on top of it, forepaws demolishing the mountains and pink tongue lolling as he panted out his excitement. There were no recriminations from Lindy. She hugged the dog ecstatically then jumped up and led him into a happy race around the trees.

Susan stood and brushed the sand from her hands. Dave was strolling down the path from the western entrance. She waved and he lifted his hand in a lazy salute. A surge of pleasure brought a smile to her face. He might look a mess but he was a rare kind of person and she liked him. Very much. She picked up her handbag and joined him as he reached his bench.

'I'm so glad you came. We've missed you,' she declared, artlessly showing her pleasure at seeing him.

He looked a little surprised. A dry smile twitched at his lips. 'Oddly enough I've found myself missing you the last few days. Must be less self-sufficient than I thought. What have you been up to?'

'Lindy was sick earlier on in the week and then I started my new job.'

'Oh yes! The job!' His smile disappeared.

Susan could feel a barrier sliding between them and suddenly it seemed terribly important to prevent that happening. She had been able to speak more openly to Dave than to anyone else in her whole life and he understood things that even Kev had not understood. 'Please don't make me feel guilty, Dave,' she said impulsively. 'What else can I do but take a job?'

He did not answer immediately and when he did it was in a mocking drawl. 'Oh, marry some rich bloke who'll take the load off your shoulders.'

'I couldn't marry just for money,' she retorted sharply, then softened her voice to appeal. 'Besides, how can I meet anyone if I stay at home?'

He turned his gaze on her, eyes teasing provocatively. 'You met me in the park. And you didn't have a job then.'

She sighed in exasperation. 'Dave, I'm very glad to have met you, but I might point out that you can't afford to keep yourself, let alone me and Lindy. Which reminds me . . .' She opened her handbag and extracted a twenty-dollar note. '. . . here's the money I owe you for the meal at McDonald's.'

He glanced down at the note and shrugged. 'Forget it. You were doing me a favour.'

'No, I wasn't. I really wanted to go. You must take it,' she insisted earnestly.

He gave her an amused look. 'It's far too much anyway and I don't have any change on me. Keep it, Susan. I don't need it.'

'Dave . . .' She hesitated, not wanting to hurt his pride but determined that he should take the money. 'Dave, will you do me a favour?'

'Probably,' he said carelessly. 'Depends on what it is, doesn't it?'

'Well, I've got a job now and I don't have to be so careful with money. I want you to take the twenty dollars, and with what's left over from the meal we had, would you go and get a haircut and a beard trim?'

He eyed her quizzically for a few moments, watching the inevitable flush of embarrassment creep up her cheeks. 'It means that much to you?' he asked on a bemused note.

'I . . . I'd like you to. That's all,' she said quietly, wanting it for his sake but knowing intuitively that he would refuse if she said so.

'Well, if you don't want to be seen with me as I am . . .'

'Oh no! I don't mind,' she protested quickly, afraid that she might have offended him. She sought for another explanation. 'But, you see, other people do, Julia . . . well, Julia saw you bring us home the other night and . . .'

'And she wasn't favourably impressed,' he mocked.

'Julia tends to judge people on appearances. Most people do, Dave. I told her you were my friend and . . .'

'But she hassled you about me.'

The grim look which settled on his face drove Susan to retract. 'Dave, I don't care. Truly, I don't. You can look any way you like and it won't matter to how I feel about you. Please . . . just forget I said anything,' she finished miserably.

Immediately his eyes softened. 'Sweet Susan. I shall not have you suffer on my account. Not in the smallest way.' He leaned over, took the twenty-dollar note from her hand and gave her a cheeky grin as he stuffed it into his pocket. 'The next time you see me I shall be respectably shorn, right up to my ear lobes. Come to think of it, I might have a mohawk cut. It'd last me longer.'

The twinkle in his eyes told her he was joking. 'Why not just leave a tonsure like a monk?' she suggested in similar vein.

'Nope! I suspect I'm too monk-like in my habits as it is. I can see it's about time I stirred myself out of them.'

A thrill of achievement added brilliance to Susan's smile. 'I think that's a good idea.'

He laughed. 'You'll have me working next. Tell me about this new job of yours.'

Careful not to discourage him from getting a job himself, Susan stressed the new experience which her work was providing. She told him about the morning's visit to the computer centre and how it had opened her eyes to the practical use of computers. This set Dave off on a long philosophical argument about human dependency on machines. Susan took issue with some of his theories and the conversation developed into a lively debate which lasted all afternoon.

Susan sighed with regret when she realised it was time to be going home. A talk with Dave was always stimulating. 'Well, no matter what you say, Dave Brown, machines are here to stay, and Lindy is going to watch one while I memorise a manual about one,' she declared as she stood up to call her daughter over.

'What manual?'

'The manual for the word-processor I have to operate at work. Since I've had a thorough demonstration, I should be able to make some orderly sense out of it now.'

'You know why they've invented word-processors? Because people don't bother learning how to spell correctly,' Dave claimed in disgust.

Susan grinned at him. 'Don't start again. Besides, the machine isn't going to rule me. I'm determined to have it mastered by Monday.'

He grinned back at her. 'I'd walk you home only I have to see a barber first.'

'You do that,' she retorted with a laugh. 'Bye for now.'

She collected Lindy from the slide and Dave whistled for Wally to come to him. It had been a very pleasant afternoon and the thought that she might have prodded Dave out of his indifference to life was particularly pleasing to Susan. She doubted that he would ever have James Kelleher's drive for success but she was sure that he could lead a more satisfying life if he wanted to.

James Kelleher was almost a different species from Dave, a man of dynamic energy and purpose, with the kind of presence which would always make him a centre of attraction. Susan felt dazzled by him, so dazzled that she had no perception of the heart of the man. She felt comfortable with Dave. She knew Dave liked her. He even cared enough about her feelings to tidy up his appearance. But James Kelleher's feelings towards her were very obscure. And tantalising.

Susan dressed with special care on Monday morning. The slimline apricot dress with its burnt orange trim was not as eye-catching as the red and white outfit she had worn on Friday so she hoped to escape Erica Ainsley's disapproval. Most of Susan's savings had gone on the clothes Julia had steered her into buying and they had to do, no matter what anyone thought.

Fortunately there were no grumbles from Lindy when Susan took her daughter up to Julia. Derek was sitting on the kitchen floor, surrounded by his vast collection of Lego blocks and Lindy eagerly joined him. Julia made a few arch remarks about chauffeurs and Susan quickly escaped, more prepared to stand at the front gate for ten minutes than to suffer her sister's teasing.

It was lucky that she had come out early since the BMW pulled into the kerb five minutes later. Susan hurried to the passenger side and James leaned across the seat to open the door for her. Heart thumping with nervous excitement, she slid into place, closed the door and threw James a shy smile.

'Thank you.'

The vivid blue eyes regarded her with friendly amusement. 'I do like punctuality in a girl. Most refreshing. And how are you this morning? Ready to fight the foe and come out winning?'

'I hope so. At least I feel prepared.' His easy manner gave her the courage to ask, 'Do you suppose Miss Ainsley will think this dress suitable?'

His gaze slid down to the quick rise and fall of her breasts underneath the soft blouson bodice.

Susan had not meant to draw attention to her body and the slight curl of James Kelleher's mouth made her very conscious of her fulsome curves. She concentrated on him in an attempt to forget herself. He wore a three-piece fawn suit this morning, cream silk shirt, silk tie; all beautifully pressed and quietly proclaiming his very executive status.

'Susan, I really don't think Erica's going to like you in any dress,' he said drily. His eyes met hers with disturbing directness. 'However, if you want my opinion, you look very suitable ... in every sense.'

Was he flirting with her? The intonation given to those last three words had been suggestive and the accompanying smile sent her pulse rate haywire. Before Susan could catch her breath to say anything James turned his attention to driving. Once they had joined the mainstream of traffic heading into the city he asked about her weekend, showing a friendly interest in her replies but nothing more than that. The occasional glance at her was almost impersonal and their inevitable parting in the office building was completely casual. Susan decided that while he might find her physically attractive, James Kelleher had no intention of becoming involved with a mere employee.

She felt flat all day, despite not putting a foot wrong as far as work was concerned. She had one secret moment of triumph when she delivered some faultless papers off the word-processor to Erica Ainsley. The woman checked the work meticulously and a certain amount of chagrin showed when she snapped a 'thank you'. The names and faces of the office people gradually became more familiar and Susan found Denise

Rowe far more friendly now that Christine was no longer present.

At four-thirty a call came through for James. She had handled several calls for him during the day and he had accepted them all in a brisk, business-like voice. The unexpected injection of warmth in his tone this time gave a lift to her heart.

'Just a moment, Susan. We'll leave at a quarter to five. Get ahead of the traffic jam if possible. Be ready for me, will you?'

'Yes, Mr Kelleher.'

He chuckled. 'How very proficient you've sounded all day!'

'And you,' she replied, made bold by his sudden levity.

'Dear Susan. I am nothing if not proficient. Four forty-five on the dot.'

'Yes, sir. Shall I put Mr Willoughby through now?'

'By all means let me have Mr Willoughby.'

She made the connection and turned to Denise, knowing that it was now unavoidable that the receptionist would learn who was giving Susan a lift during the train strike. It had probably been foolish of her not to reveal James Kelleher's kindness but she had suspected that Denise might carry on like Julia, and Susan had not wanted to be the object of such speculation here in the office.

'Denise, I have to leave at a quarter to five. Will you handle any calls after that?'

'No worries. My boyfriend's not picking me up until five-thirty. We decided to take in a show and let all the others crawl home first. There are some advantages to train strikes,' she added with a smug little smile.

A mixture of cowardice and self-consciousness

held Susan's tongue silent. Denise would surely think James Kelleher was a fantastic advantage. Which he was. A spine-tingling excitement confirmed that. At twenty to five Susan darted into the rest room to freshen her lipstick. To her dismay she found a tight-lipped Erica Ainsley impatiently waiting on her return.

'Get a dozen copies of these run off before five o'clock,' she ordered icily, thrusting a manila folder into Susan's hands.

James Kelleher picked that moment to enter the reception area. Susan looked at him helplessly, the folder a loadstone of duty which demanded she stay at work.

'Ready?' he asked, flashing a smile which encompassed Denise and Erica Ainsley.

Heat scorched into Susan's cheeks. 'Please ... please excuse me, Mr Kelleher. I can't leave until ... until I've completed some work for Miss Ainsley. I'll catch a bus.'

'Nonsense! There's nothing that can't wait until the morning.' He cocked a sardonic eyebrow at the rigid Miss Ainsley. 'Isn't that so, Erica? We must make these time allowances during train strikes. I'm providing Miss Hardy with transport during the present emergency and we're leaving now. Come, Susan. Put down the folder, pick up your handbag and move, my girl. I refuse to be delayed.'

Susan obeyed, conscious of bristling hostility from the older woman and breathless astonishment from Denise. Without daring to glance at either of them she muttered an awkward apology and followed James who had swept through to the corridor leading to the lifts. As she stepped into the compartment he had held waiting, James Kelleher threw her a grin of gloating triumph. The doors closed behind her and he leaned back against the wall, blue eyes still dancing with intense satisfaction.

'I do relish the role of St George. Any more dragons you'd like me to slay?'

She sighed. 'Mr Kelleher . . .'

'James.'

'James.' She smiled. He was quite irresistible. 'I suspect I shall pay for your rescue operation, but thank you all the same.'

'So you should. I believe the traditional payment for a knight in shining armour is a chaste kiss.'

Her startled look provoked a peal of merriment. The lift doors opened on to the basement car park and, still chuckling to himself, James steered Susan out, hand lightly pressing on the small of her back.

'What's so funny?' she asked.

'Me. You. You have an extraordinary effect on me and I can't help but think how absurd it is.'

'What's absurd? Your giving an employee a lift home in your car?'

'Oh no! Not even Erica could make a valid objection to that.' They had reached the BMW and James unlocked the passenger door and swung it open. His smile had a twist of irony as he took in the bewilderment on her face. 'You put me at odds with myself. Something no other woman has ever achieved, Miss Susan Hardy. And the absurdity is in the fact that a girl like you can exert such an influence on me, of all men. You'd better hop in before I do something I'll be sure to regret.'

With a little shake of her head which expressed her total incomprehension, Susan slid into the passenger seat. She mused on his puzzling words until the BMW was wedged into a relentless line of traffic. Then feeling distinctly unsure that he even wanted her in his car, Susan could remain silent no longer.

'Please don't feel obliged to go out of your way on my account. I don't want to be any trouble to you. I can get to work by myself tomorrow.'

He glanced at her in surprise. 'It's no trouble.' His eyebrows rose quizzically. 'What are you worrying about now?'

'You said I made you feel at odds with yourself.'

'So you do,' he tossed at her lightly, and grinned at her confusion. 'I'm not a man of impulse. Normally it would not occur to me to interfere with Erica's choice of a job candidate. I acted on impulse, just as I acted on impulse in asking you to dine with me last Friday night. That's not to say I've regretted either impulse, but ... let's just say that the evening I spent with you was uncharacteristic of any evening I've spent with a woman.'

He slanted her a smile which smacked of self-mockery. 'I don't normally deny myself anything I want. Nor have I ever felt protective towards the female sex. It's rather odd to discover a hitherto untapped sense of chivalry in myself. A new experience. Quite intriguing and possibly dangerous to my peace of mind if I'm not careful.'

The teasing sparkle in his eyes denied the words any real weight. Susan smiled, relieved to know that everything was all right. Better than all right. He was virtually saying that she was something special in his experience of women and that thought gave an exultant lift to her spirits. He was special too. Maybe too special for her.

'I enjoyed the evening, too,' she said, then defensively played down the too-eager note in her voice by adding, 'I imagine any girl would enjoy an evening out with you.'

'You're feeding my ego,' he said derisively.

She sighed, perversely wishing that he was not quite so devastatingly attractive. It made all things possible for him and, however special he might consider her, Susan felt that a country girl would not hold any lasting attraction for him.

'That was my first visit to a fancy restaurant,' she admitted. It was no use pretending a sophistication she did not have. She could not match his experience.

His look was curiously speculative. 'I would never have guessed.'

'I'm glad it didn't show. You must be used to ... oh, all sorts of fancy social occasions. The best places ... and the best people.'

'Fashionable and influential, perhaps. Not necessarily the best. And one can get very bored with what are supposedly the best places and people. The label has a price,' he added drily.

'Would you wish your life any different?'

A red traffic light had halted them. He turned to her, blue eyes suddenly sharp with a hunger which seemed to draw on her very soul. 'Sometimes. Sometimes I wonder if the price is too high.' The car behind them blew its horn and James's attention snapped back to the road. 'But only sometimes,' he muttered as he nudged the BMW forward. 'Do you have any ambitions, Susan?' he asked in a more casual tone.

'Not in any career sense.'

'To travel the world and see all there is to be seen?'

She laughed. 'Give me a chance. I've only just taken the gigantic step out of one small town to a big city.'

He slanted her a wry little smile. 'Well, I hope you find what you want.'

'I don't want very much. Yet I suppose you could say I want everything that really matters.'

'And what really matters to you?'

The amused tone in his voice made her hesitate, but a sense of pride, of conviction in her own beliefs forced out the truth she would not deny. 'Love. To love and be loved,' she said softly.

He answered her with hard cynicism. 'Love is an illusion, my dear Susan. The substance of dreams. Too ephemeral to sacrifice what's real for it.'

'Then you've never known it, James, or you couldn't say that. It's worth any sacrifice.'

He raised his eyebrows at her. The quiet dignity of certain knowledge shone from her dark eyes. He shrugged and returned his gaze to the road ahead, a slight curl on his lips.

'And you have known love,' he said sardonically.

'Yes.'

'What? The love of your parents, no doubt.'

'Yes.' And more. Much more. But she did not want to risk James's scoffing at the love she and Kev had shared.

'I suppose you miss them,' he said more kindly.

'I do, but I know it's time that I learnt to be independent of them. After all, I am twenty-one.'

He flashed her an indulgent smile. 'A grand old age.'

'It may not seem so to you, James. Even so, I feel I've lived one lifetime. Since I came to the city, another has begun.' She sighed and added ruefully, 'It's new and strange and I feel very unsure of my place in it.'

'Are you regretting the move?'

'No. It was necessary.'

'Why necessary? That's a rather emphatic word,' he commented curiously.

But it had been necessary. For her sake. For Lindy's sake. To find love. Lamamby held no promise of that any more.

'You're not a criminal on the run,' James threw at her jokingly.

She laughed. 'No. Nothing like that. I'm a very law-abiding citizen.'

'Never put a foot wrong in your life,' he teased.

'I put every possible foot wrong last Friday, but at least I got through today without a blunder,' she said with satisfaction.

'I knew you'd come up trumps. My instinct for winners never lies.'

A slight break in the traffic enabled a quick turn into Julia's street. They had made reasonably good time despite the clogged state of the road. It was not yet five-thirty, much earlier than Susan had expected to be home. As the BMW pulled up parallel to the house she spotted Julia in the front garden, directing a hose on to the rose bed.

Susan wondered if her sister had deliberately timed this chore to coincide with her home-coming. The lure of seeing James Kelleher in the flesh would be irresistible to Julia. She just had to know everything. Predictably her head turned their way as the BMW pulled into the kerb.

'Your sister?' James asked with a knowing smile.

Of course he would know why Julia had stationed herself in the garden. 'Yes,' Susan sighed. 'Thanks again, James. Do you think the train strike will be over tonight?'

'Not a chance. Same time tomorrow morning?'

'I'll be ready,' she promised him and quickly let herself out of the car, not wanting to give Julia the opportunity of making her curiosity too obvious. Besides, it saved time for James if he stayed behind the wheel.

'Mummy! Mummy!' Shrieking with delight, Lindy came hurtling out to greet her.

Susan swiftly pushed the passenger door shut and bent down to scoop her daughter up into her arms. 'Lindy, you mustn't run on to the road. You didn't even look for cars,' she scolded.

'Yes, I did, Mummy. I've been looking at every car that's come. And I saw you first,' Lindy declared smugly.

'Well, next time wait on the pavement for me. Promise?'

'Okay. I promise.'

Susan was extremely conscious of James's listening presence and the softly idling engine of the BMW. He should have gone. There was no reason for him to still be here. She turned to find him staring at her, stunned disbelief in the vivid blue eyes.

She heaved a sigh of resignation. If Lindy's existence shocked him then it was just too bad. A man who could not accept her daughter was of no use to Susan. But it hurt to realise that Lindy could form an impediment to a developing relationship. And it had been developing. Up until this moment. But now? Well, she would know tomorrow.

She lifted her hand in a dismissive wave. James reacted slowly, his gaze stabbing from mother to daughter and back again. He returned her salute as if in a daze, then abruptly jerked his head away, a heavy frown creasing his forehead. The engine roared. The car accelerated forward. Too fast for a suburban street. Swiftly ending something that hadn't quite begun? She would know tomorrow.

James called love an illusion, but it wasn't. It was real. As real as the daughter in her arms. Whom she loved with all her heart. Giving the little girl a fiercely possessive hug, Susan walked over to Julia.

'He had to know, Suz,' her sister said softly, showing a surprising depth of understanding. 'Better for him to know now.'

Susan nodded.

'Not that anyone wouldn't want both of you,' Julia added with a bright smile of reassurance.

Susan shrugged away any speculation. 'I'm not sure he even wants one of us.' Her smile was dismissive and for once, Julia didn't pursue an argument.

CHAPTER FIVE

JAMES arrived early. Even earlier than yesterday. Susan was just stepping off the front patio when the BMW drew to a halt. She sucked in a deep breath, willed her treacherous blood circulation not to pound her cheeks in its usual extravagant manner and, with her head held at a proud, independent angle, she walked towards the car, determined not to be flustered no matter what James said. If indeed he said anything. It was more probable that he would ignore yesterday altogether and distance himself to a firm employer/employee footing.

'Good morning!' His door was open and in one fluid movement James was on his feet. His smile was one of undiluted pleasure. 'You look even more beautiful in blue.'

The compliment undermined her careful composure and the smile demolished it. Of all the outfits she had bought the blue was her favourite and she had worn the tailored blouse and skirt this morning as a confidence-booster. With one sentence James had boosted much more than her confidence.

'I'm glad you think so.' The happy lilt of her voice matched her responding smile as she was ushered into the car.

James swiftly returned to his own side but he did not start the engine. He looked at her with warmly caressing eyes. 'Why didn't you tell me you had an equally beautiful daughter?'

His directness peeled away the defences she had

erected and she looked back at him with hopelessly vulnerable eyes. 'Lindy is a very personal part of my life. Not the kind of subject for idle curiosity, James.'

'Not idle, Susan. I don't feel the least bit idle about you,' he said softly. He reached across and gently stroked her cheek. 'You have known love, haven't you? And pain. Do you know, I'm envious of you.'

Her breath was caught somewhere in the back of her throat but she managed to gasp out, 'Envious? Of me?' It seemed incredible. This man who had everything. Yet she sensed the hunger in him and her heart galloped wildly at the thought that he wanted her to appease it.

His hand dropped to her lap where it took one of her hands and fondled it in a curious, exploratory way. His thumb drew over the lifelines in her palm while he spoke in a low, musing tone. 'I wonder what it would be like to let go. Do something completely unplanned, reckless. To follow emotion instead of ambition.' His gaze lifted to hers, intensely probing. 'Is the world well lost for love, Susan?'

She swallowed to moisten her dry throat. The question demanded a serious answer. 'I can't speak for you, James. I only know that, for me, life would be very meaningless without it.'

'Meaningless.' He repeated the word as if tasting it, feeling out his reaction. 'No, not meaningless. Shallow, perhaps. And I would like to know what the depths hold. To at least experience what I'm ...' His mouth clamped down on what he would have said, his lips thinning into a determined line before twisting into a wary smile. 'You disturb me, Susan. I went home yesterday and couldn't get you out of my mind. You and your daughter.'

He sighed and leaned back in his seat. He did not let go of Susan's hand but his hold became less gentle. His fingers dragged at the soft skin as if probing for what lay underneath. She stared at the handsome profile, amazed and deeply gratified that she could have appealed so strongly to this man who could surely have any woman.

He suddenly glanced down at their hands and gave a short laugh. 'Holding hands like a schoolboy!' He lifted his face and grinned across at her. 'I'm off my brain, Susan, but to hell with being sensible. Will you come home with me tonight? To my place where we can talk in complete privacy for as long as we like.'

Her heart gave an excited leap. 'Tonight? Or do you mean straight after work?'

'Straight from the office. Can you arrange it with your sister to look after ... what's your daughter's name again?'

'Lindy. Belinda really.'

'Pretty name. Pretty girl.' He smiled and the warmth of it was incredibly seductive. 'But tonight I want you all to myself.

The intimate purr of his voice sent a tingle of excitement racing through her veins. 'I think it will be all right. I'll ring Julia when we get to work and let you know.'

'Go in and ask her now.'

Susan shook her head. 'I've said goodbye to Lindy. I don't want to unsettle her by reappearing.'

He nodded but the warmth was abruptly withdrawn. A frown of calculation took its place. He darted her a measuring look. 'I want our association kept completely private, Susan. I lead a public enough life as it is and I dislike having my personal relationships bandied around. Office gossip . . .'

She smiled reassurance. 'I can do without that sort of talk too, James. Erica Ainsley warned me that your father frowned on any relationships between the professional and supporting staff. I don't want to make trouble at work for you or for me.'

'Erica told you that?' His surprise broke into a short, cynical laugh. 'That's Erica, all right. Covering all contingencies. I've probably made life awkward at the office for you as it is.' He sighed and slanted her a smile which dismissed all such difficulties. 'But I'll make it all up to you, Susan.'

'Don't worry about me. I can cope,' she said with all the buoyant confidence his declared interest had given her.

His eyes gloated over her. 'I wish we could take the day off. The hours won't be able to go fast enough.' His grin was touchingly boyish. 'See what you do to me? We'd better get going or I'll really lose my head.'

Susan laughed as he started the car and accelerated down the street with youthful exuberance. Her head was dizzy from the sheer speed with which nervous tension had been replaced with exhilaration. She had prepared herself to meet everything from criticism to polite indifference and she was astonished, delighted and immensely flattered by James's spontaneous outburst of feeling. Feeling towards her. It was wonderful to know, to be really sure that his interest was personal and very genuine.

The hours did not drag for Susan. The day flew by on the wings of glorious anticipation. Once she had Julia's assurance that Lindy would be well cared for, not even Erica Ainsley's sour sniping or Denise's pestering curiosity could dim her inner elation. Whenever she put through a call to James he made some deliciously personal remark which increased her light-headedness. It was a major miracle that she had enough concentration left to perform her job with the efficiency required to avoid critical comment.

As for avoiding gossip, it was fortunate that Susan was the only person in the reception area when James came to collect her at the end of the day. She could not have disguised her excitement. Nor did James attempt to disguise his pleasure at seeing her. He took her hand and the warm strength of his touch vibrated right up her arm, electrifying the thought that tonight he would kiss her. Kiss her properly.

Nothing of consequence was said on their drive out of the city. The mood in the car was one of barely suppressed excitement which bubbled out into light-hearted banter. Their eyes said what did not need to be put into words. This was a voyage of discovery, important to both of them, and the night ahead was theirs to make of it what they could, each looking for and hoping to find answers to their needs.

James's home was a penthouse apartment in Roseville. It had its own private garage and private lift. All of which impressed on Susan just how wealthy the man had to be, a far cry from her own circumstances. The comparison jarred on her but James seemed to take pleasure in pointing out the luxuries of life which were his to enjoy. And hers. For tonight.

Oddly enough, for all the obvious expensiveness of the apartment's furnishings, Susan thought they lacked personality and homeliness. She felt each room was a set, ready to be photographed for an interior decorator's magazine. The black leather armchairs looked cold, arranged as they were around glass and chrome occasional tables. The thick, off-white carpet appeared far too pristine to be walked upon and the modern, surrealistic paintings on the walls seemed bleak and soulless.

'Like it?' James asked confidently.

'Fastastic!' she replied. Quite truthfully. It was too fantastic to picture herself readily at home here.

James headed for the bar which occupied an alcove off the living-room. He casually discarded his jacket, tie and waistcoat, and rolled up his shirtsleeves. As he undid half the shirt buttons to reveal a smooth, golden-tan chest, his face relaxed into a satisfied grin.

'It's great to shrug off the professional image. Every damned image. Tonight I'm going to be free of it all. You make that possible, Susan, and I'm going to relish every moment of it.'

Susan seated herself on a bar stool and regarded him curiously. 'Don't you relax like this very often?'

'By myself, yes. Not with others.'

'Why not?'

'Because, dear Susan, one of the golden rules of competition is, never give away an advantage by revealing a weakness. One must step warily and wisely if one wishes to advance to the top.'

'The top of what? The law-courts?'

He laughed and shook his head as he bent to draw a tray of ice-cubes out of the bar refrigerator. 'Law is only a step along the way. Politics is where the power is. I'm heading for parliament at the next election. A blue-ribbon seat if all goes as planned.'

'I'm afraid I know nothing of politics, James,' Susan said anxiously, more and more aware of how little they had in common.

'Which makes you even more attractive to me. I'm up to my ears in it most of the time. I need an escape-valve, someone with whom I can be myself,' he declared with a smile which chased away her uncertainties. 'Now, what would you like to drink?'

'A long, cold, lemon squash, please.'

He cocked a quizzical eyebrow at her. 'You wouldn't like something more adventurous?'

She shrugged. 'I know I like lemon squash.'

He laughed and proceeded to make her drink and another for himself with whisky and dry ginger ale. 'Let's go out to the balcony. We can enjoy the fresh, evening breeze and watch the lights of the city switch on.'

Susan slid off her stool and winced as her feet took her weight again. 'James, since we're relaxing, would you mind terribly much if I took my shoes off? My feet are still protesting the necessity of wearing high-heeled shoes all day long.'

'By all means remove them. Your stockings, too. Take off anything that will make you feel more comfortable.'

'I might do that,' she muttered, wriggling her freed toes in the soft carpet. The nylon tights did feel sticky on her thighs. For a moment she thought of Dave and his objection to nylon shirts. With a slight smile twitching at the memory she lifted her gaze to James. 'Would you point me to the bathroom?'

He smiled. 'Wouldn't you like to tease me by taking them off here?'

The provocative gleam in his eyes and the sexual innuendo brought an instant flush to Susan's cheeks. She stepped back from him, offended that he should think she had any such intention.

'I'm sorry,' he sighed, and placed the drinks

down on the bar. Then he was gathering her into a
gentle embrace and his eyes held a wry softness.
'You have no guile in you at all, have you, Susan?
I like that. I really do. It means that I can trust
you. And the people you can trust are few and far
between in this dog-eat-dog world. I am very lucky
to have found you.' One hand lifted and cupped
her cheek, his thumb lightly tilting her chin. 'And
you're so very beautiful.'

As he had done before, he bent his head and
brushed her lips with a tantalising kiss. But not
once. Again and again while he pulled her closer,
pressing, moulding her lower body to his, forcing a
gradual awareness of contoured flesh and hard
muscle which was totally sensual. So beguiled was
she by the physical sensations he was arousing that
the quick flick of his tongue between her lips
surprised her into opening her mouth. Then she
was too fascinated by a whole new range of
feelings to even think of resistance to such
unaccustomed intimacy.

Exploration quickly accelerated into a whirling
urgency which sought a greater depth of satisfaction. With increasing passion their mouths worked
to feed a hunger which fed on itself. Susan had
never been kissed with such devouring intensity.
When James reverted to soft, feathery kisses across
her throbbing lips, she remained dazed by the
strength of her reaction.

She sucked in a shuddering breath and opened
her eyes. She found her fingers still thrust into the
wavy thickness of hair at the back of James' neck.
With a shocked thump she landed back on her
heels. James lifted his head and Susan quickly
dropped her hands to the front of his shirt. She
stared up at him, confused and a little ashamed of
her abandoned response. The blue eyes were hazy

with sensual satisfaction which did nothing at all
to calm Susan's pulse rate.

'You ... you were going to show me where ...
where the bathroom is,' she stammered, in an
effort to collect her wits.

'So I was.' The husky purr of his voice was like
a shivery caress on her skin.

'Please ...' It embarrassed her to hear a hint of
panic in her voice. It seemed so gauche to feel
panicky over a kiss but she had not expected to
lose control of her senses. And she had.

James's hands slid down and gripped her waist,
almost spanning it, an act of possession. His gaze
dropped to her still heaving breasts, lingering
there, seemingly reluctant to release the hold he
had undoubtedly had on her. 'You have a very
womanly body, Susan. Soft. Yielding. Don't ever
let anyone persuade you to diet down to skin and
bone.' He lifted his face and smiled. 'The
bathroom's down the hall. Second door on the
right.'

He let her go. Susan found the bathroom and
set about reducing her highly flustered state,
splashing her hot face with cold water and holding
her wrists under the running tap. Well, she had
wanted to know what it would be like to be kissed
by James Kelleher and now she knew, Susan told
her wide-eyed reflection in the mirror. And how! It
was the most composure-shattering kiss she had
ever experienced. Not even Kev had ever kissed
her like that. Their youthful passion had not
known such devastating expertise. Emotion had
driven them into lovemaking, not the physical
seduction of their senses.

It alarmed her to think she could so easily
become intoxicated by James's sexual artistry,
because that was what it was, a consummate

knowledge of how to arouse and draw a response.
After all, she did not know him well enough to
love him. He was a handsome, exciting man but,
despite having learnt something about him, Susan
felt that the inner person still escaped her. All the
attraction was really on the surface, a very brilliant
surface which tended to distract her from looking
beyond it.

She turned off the taps and dried her hands. Her
initial reason for coming to the bathroom was to
remove her tights but now she hesitated over doing
so. What had seemed quite natural before James's
kiss could now be misinterpreted as an invitation
for sexual play and that was not what she had in
mind at all. On the other hand, having declared
her intention of taking them off, not to do so
would telegraph to James that she was more
disturbed than she wanted him to know. She took
them off, rolled them up and thrust them into her
handbag. With composure restored and coolly
bare-legged she returned to the living-room.

The measured tone of a newsreader came
through an archway. Susan picked up her drink
from the bar and padded across the thick carpet,
listening to the voice becoming more distinct.

'. . . running normally from midnight tonight.
And now for the sporting news, I'll pass you over
to . . .'

James switched off the radio just as Susan
entered the kitchen. He had changed his clothes
and his physical beauty was even more noticeable,
the lithe, muscular physique revealed and emphasised by the blue sports shirt and white shorts.

He flashed her a smile. 'Feeling better?'

'Yes, thank you. Any news about the train
strike?'

'They're going back to work tonight. Pity the

union has been so reasonable for once. It would raise too many eyebrows if I kept driving you to and from the office, Susan, but we'll find time to get together after hours. As much time as possible,' he added with fervour.

The possessive gleam in his eyes left Susan in no doubt that he meant it. It was strange that instead of feeling flattered she felt slightly apprehensive. She shrugged off the absurdity and asked impulsively, 'Can I help you?'

James was taking a selection of cheeses out of the refrigerator. The kitchen was brown and white and very modern, so streamlined that Susan wondered if it was ever put to much use. There was no spice-jars or cannisters or any kitchen-ware on show.

'Nothing much to do,' he replied. 'I thought we'd have something to nibble on with our drinks. Just have to get some crackers out of the pantry.'

He folded back the doors at the far end of the kitchen, revealing a well set-up work area with all practical appliances and closely stocked shelves running up the walls. Having removed a box of crackers, James re-closed the doors, neatly restoring the streamlined look. It struck Susan forcefully that the whole apartment was a façade, a streamlined façade which was characteristic of James himself. To get to know the man she had to persuade him to open the doors into his mind.

She suspected that he only ever did so for a set purpose. Just as he had opened the pantry only long enough to get the crackers, he had revealed only enough of himself this morning to persuade Susan into coming home with him. Well, she was here now and surely, in the long evening ahead of them, he would relax his guard more and more, and her view of him would become clearer.

They moved out on to the balcony and settled on to vinyl-cushioned armachairs with matching footstools. The city stretched out below them, filling every horizon in sight.

'I like it up here. Always wanted to be king of the castle when I was a kid,' James remarked with a cheeky grin.

'And were you?' He had given her an opening.

'Most of the time, I guess.' His eyes twinkled devilment. 'Comes with having the gift of the gab. Always could talk my way out of trouble and into the front line of favour.'

She smiled. 'A very useful gift. Tell me about your life, James. All I know is that you're a successful barrister. What about everything that led up to now?'

Urged on by her eager questions James revealed that he had indeed been king of a long line of castles: captain of the cricket team, captain of the football team, school captain, president of the students' union at university, editor of the campus newspaper, prize-winning law graduate.

His natural ability, allied to a keen, competitive spirit, had brought him many laurels and a burning ambition for more shone through every word. It wasn't enough to be good. He had to be the best at whatever he attempted and Susan had to admire his drive and application. With his looks and natural talents it would have been quite easy to coast along at a higher level than most people achieved, but James had scorned the easy path.

'You make me feel ashamed,' she commented ruefully. 'I've never really pushed myself to achieve anything. Oh, I've done as well as I could at anything I've undertaken, but I haven't gone out of my way to excel. I've always tried to fit in rather than shine out.'

'And that's part of your charm,' he said with warm approval. 'You wouldn't ever think of grinding others down. You care more for others than yourself, don't you, Susan? You worry about how they think, what they feel. You want to make them happy.'

She laughed self-consciously. 'I'm not quite as unselfish as that, James.'

The warmth in his eyes deepened. 'You are beautiful. Not only to look at but to be with. So receptive and undemanding. I find no spite in you, no envy, no greed.'

'For goodness sake! Don't make me out to be a saint.'

'Not a saint. A woman worth having.'

Her heart stopped, then catapulted around her chest, leaping towards the concentrated power in those vivid blue eyes and retreating to the insistent beat of caution in her brain.

He stood up, took her hands and slowly drew her to her feet. Susan trembled under his touch, a light, caressing touch which explored the curves of her body with a deliberation which was oddly mesmerising. His eyes burnt into hers, wanting all she had to give, melting her resistance.

'Don't be frightened. I'm not playing with you, Susan,' he assured her softly. 'I value you very highly, enough to give you and your daughter all the security you could ever want. So long as I'm the man you want.'

Very gently he kissed her eyes shut, closing off the feverish questions before he took seductive possession of her mouth, not intent on passion but on persuasion, not so much arousing excitement as appeasing any doubts of his sincerity. His tender loving was so pleasant that Susan sighed with regret when it ended.

'I think this can best be continued later,' James murmured huskily. 'It's well past time for some dinner. Shall we go inside and get ourselves a meal?'

'Yes. Good idea,' she agreed breathlessly.

He was sweeping her along so fast she could do with a breathing space. The mundane chore of preparing something to eat would give her time to get her feet back on the ground. It seemed incredible that James could seriously be thinking of marriage to her at this early stage of their relationship, yet what else could he mean by offering her and Lindy lifelong security? She felt positively overwhelmed by the idea. James, in love with her?

Between them they prepared an appetising salad. Hunger demanded that she eat but Susan scarcely tasted a thing. She felt quite intoxicated and the wine James kept pouring for her did nothing to clear her head. Never in her wildest dreams had she imagined a man like James Kelleher coming into her life, let alone his considering that she, Susan Hardy, was the woman he wanted above all others.

In an attempt to get some bearings on reality she asked him about his family. It was a family full of distinguished careers on both sides but James himself was an only child. Susan wondered how acceptable she would be to a mother and father who would always have expected the best for such a son. The only son. And heir. Apparently to a very considerable fortune.

Then she decided that James was not a man to be swayed from his course. Once he had determined upon something he carried it through. Everything he had told her about himself confirmed that strength of character. He would

win through sheer indomitable will, if that was
possible. If he decided upon her as his wife, then it
followed that Susan was right for him.

But was he right for her? And Lindy? Such a
question seemed stupid in the face of all that he
was and all that he had to offer her, but still it
niggled at the edges of her dazed mind. While all
the time his eyes kept reinforcing the intoxicating
message that she was uniquely desirable.

They sat talking over the dinner table for a long
time. At least James talked. Susan listened, her
infatuation growing by the minute. He had met so
many interesting people, important people, and
while his comments on them sometimes had a
cynical flavour, she was too fascinated by the
range of public personages involved to attach any
significance to James's view of them.

'Enough of other people. Tonight there's only
us. Let's go and listen to some music. I'm tired of
talking. You're too good a listener, Susan,' he
admonished her teasingly as he drew back his
chair and rose from the table.

'I love listening to you,' she answered artlessly.

'I'd prefer you to love me,' he murmured in her
ear as he helped her out of her chair.

Susan blushed. James laughed and brushed one
hot cheek with his knuckles before sliding an arm
around her shoulders and leading her into the
living-room. He left her to settle into one of the
leather armchairs while he set a tape going on the
hi-fi set. The muted strains of a symphony
orchestra provided pleasant music which required
no comment. Susan relaxed, supremely content
with the moment.

Instead of taking a chair James sprawled on to
the carpet and leant his head back against her seat
cushion. He lifted her legs over his shoulder so

that her feet landed in his lap. Strong fingers massaged toes which had lost their cramp hours ago.

He threw her a grin. 'I bet you're a good athlete.'

'Why? Because I have long legs?' she asked, aware of a ripple of excitement running up the whole length of them.

'No. Your second toe is markedly longer than your big toe. See?' He waggled them teasingly.

'So?' She tried to wriggle the ultra-sensitivity out of her feet.

'Sign of a top runner. They all have long second toes.'

She laughed. 'I think you're kidding me but it's true that I can run well. I used to win races at school.'

'There you are. Proof! Mine are the same. See?'

He kicked off his plimsolls and Susan leaned forward to look. Instantly James' arms reached up, caught her and hoisted her down to the floor, flat on her back with the breath knocked out of her.

'That's not fair!' she gasped in protest.

He leaned over her, eyes laughing in triumph. 'But much more convenient. I would've got a stiff neck looking up at you, and however shapely your legs, they weren't quite enough to satisfy my lust to see all of you.'

His gaze travelled down her body to where her skirt had rucked up. Before she could grasp his intention, tantalising fingers trailed up her soft, inner thigh to the elastic legband of her bikini pants. Nerve-endings screeched alarm and Susan jack-knifed forward to snatch the offending hand away. But it was gone before she reached it. James' arms encircled her body and she was lowered to the floor again, and his mouth was on hers, offering the sensual temptation of its possession. Susan did not resist it. Did not want to.

Nevertheless she bucked an instinctive protest when a hard-muscled thigh moved her legs apart. Her hand tried to restrain his from unbuttoning her blouse and snapping open the front fastening of her bra, but he was strong and the unrelenting passion of his kisses had infiltrated her muscles with an aching weakness.

Her breast was bared, the rounded flesh softly kneaded, her nipple teased erect by an insistent thumb. A chaos of sensations burst into life, driving her heart-beat faster, louder, making her whole body pulse with excitement. Her mind was drowned by a shattering cry of physical need and when James' mouth moved down to capture her breast and his hand once more reached for intimate exploration, only a moan of desire whispered across her lips.

The telephone rang. Its shrill, repetitive summons broke into the sexual thrall which had sapped Susan's will. A spurt of adrenalin brought agitated strength to her arms and she pushed at James, trying to lift him away.

'Please stop,' she whispered hoarsely.

His mouth released her throbbing breast and he rested his head just below her throat. 'Hush! It's all right,' he soothed, and his hand stroked up across her rounded stomach, easing some of the tension he had so skilfully built.

The ringing stopped. James heaved himself up, then bent to help Susan who was scrambling to her feet and trying to catch her clothes together at the same time. She stood shaking in his grasp, unable to control the aftermath of fever-pitch arousal.

'Come into the bedroom. This is no place for . . .'

'No!' she cried in panic, knowing such a move could only have one conclusion. She was not ready to surrender herself to him, not in her right mind.

He pushed her scrabbling fingers away from her bra and cupped her full breasts in his hands, pressing the advantage of her semi-nakedness. 'Susan, I want you. You want me. What's the point in denying what we both want?' he argued persuasively. 'Come on now. We can satisfy each other in absolute comfort.'

Her limbs felt like jelly but she pulled his hands away and held them down with the strength of desperation. She lifted an agonised face to his. 'James, please . . . I don't want to get pregnant.'

'Oh hell!' he breathed in frustration. 'Aren't you prepared against that?'

'No.' She shook her head frantically, hoping he would accept the excuse without argument.

He sighed and made a wry grimace. 'I haven't anything handy, either. What a bloody nuisance! We could still . . . no, dammit! It's not enough.'

'I'm sorry, James,' Susan said shakily, knowing that she had let him go too far for a refusal to be gracefully accepted. But it hadn't been all her fault.

'So you should be,' he muttered, but his tone carried resignation, not resentment.

The crisis had been safely negotiated. Susan was so grateful to be let off without any acrimony on his side that she was content to stand passively while James refastened her bra and slowly buttoned her blouse. Little shivers were still running over her skin and she sagged against him when he draw her into a comforting embrace.

'Perhaps I'd better take you home. Remove

temptation,' he murmured with a lilt of wry whimsy.

'Yes,' she agreed, trying not to sound too eager. His chest lifted and fell in a heavy sigh and his arms tightened their hold, imprinting his body on hers. 'Susan ... Susan ... let's have tomorrow night together. I'll take good care that you don't get pregnant,' he promised, his voice husky with desire.

Panic ripped through her. She needed time. It was too soon for so complete a commitment. She did not want to be rushed. She had to feel it was right, not some mad, physical compulsion. It had been years before she and Kev had consummated their love and James wanted her tomorrow night! But if she refused ... From her response tonight he had the right to expect her compliance ... She did not want to turn him away from her but ... oh, God! What was she to do?

Then on a wave of relief she remembered her bargain with Julia and saw the way to ease her problem. She pushed away from James enough to look up in appeal. 'I can't come here tomorrow night, James. I promised my sister to mind her children in return for minding Lindy tonight. You could keep me company if you like,' she invited. The possibility of being interrupted by children would surely dissuade him from any thoughts of intimacy and they could talk, be together. He could meet Lindy.

'Child-minding! That'd only be more frustration,' he declared irritably. 'Can't you get out of it? I'll pay for a baby-sitter.'

Susan felt a sharp stab of disappointment. The plan had its merits and she did not want to give it up. 'I shouldn't shrug off my responsibilities, James. Julia's been very good to me, and Lindy would be very unhappy about my deserting her two nights in a row. I thought ...' She hesitated, then plunged on hopefully. 'I thought you might like to meet Lindy.'

He sighed and smoothed away the anxiety line on her forehead. 'All I can think of is you.'

'Lindy's part of me, James,' she reminded him seriously.

'I know. I know. Another time, Susan. The hell of it is, I'm committed elsewhere until after the weekend. Monday. Can you arrange to have Monday night free? God knows I'll need you by then.'

The pressing urgency in his voice would not easily accept another refusal, and Monday was almost a week away. And she would see him, speak to him at the office. Surely by Monday she should have sorted out her feelings.

'Yes. I'm sure that will be all right.'

'Monday,' he breathed in satisfaction, then gave her a wry smile. 'My patience is going to be sorely tried, my love.' He trailed a finger around the outline of her mouth before kissing the tingling sensation away. 'I think I'd better take you home now before we tempt fate. You're very addictive, Susan Hardy.'

It was only a short drive back to Lane Cove. James saw Susan safely to her door, kissed her once more and reluctantly let her go. Confused and still physically disturbed by the sexual arousal James could excite at will, Susan trailed off to bed, not knowing if she regretted her lonely bed or welcomed it.

CHAPTER SIX

'YOU'RE crazy for even hesitating, Suz. A man like James Kelleher . . . how old is he anyway?'

'Thirty-two.'

'Well, a man of that age is not going to pussy-foot around you, holding off while you dither. My God! With his looks and wealth, he's probably had every girl he fancied falling into bed with him since his teens. If you refuse again, you'll be turning him away. Do you want to risk that? What more could you want in a man, for heaven's sake?'

The strong exasperation in Julia's voice made Susan shrink inside. 'I want to feel . . . what I felt with Kèv,' she said in a very small voice, knowing now that it had been a mistake to confide in her sister.

'Oh, Suz! You've simply got to grow up and leave the past behind,' Julia said with more sympathy. She sighed and adopted the tone of reason. 'Look! You were young, very young then, and full of romantic dreams. What you had with Kev will never be repeated. Time moves on. Whatever you have with another man will be different. You can't expect it to be the same. There'll be no one else you will have grown up with like Kev.'

Had it only been familiarity, that sense of belonging with Kev? No. No, it had been much more than that. And it hadn't been romantic dreams either. Julia was wrong on that score, but maybe she was right about love being different with another man. Susan respected James, admired him, and was most definitely attracted to him physically. But still the instinct to hold back was very strong. Perhaps it was a foolish instinct, but she could not ignore it.

'Susan . . .'

The full name was a demand for attention. Susan looked up into Julia's eyes and saw a slight evasiveness there as if her sister was not completely sure that what she wanted to say was wise, but the firm line of her mouth showed a determination to say it.

'Susan . . .'

Again the full name. It was serious all right. Susan automatically braced herself.

'. . . I'm probably going to shock you, but you've got to see reason instead of judging on emotion. You can't always trust emotions. They can change after it's too late to do anything.' Julia drew in a deep breath and plunged on. 'Look at it this way. What have you got to lose by going to bed with him? You're not a virgin. He knows you're not a virgin.'

Fire leapt to Susan's cheeks and hissed off her tongue. 'I've never been with anyone but Kev. And I loved Kev, Julia. Body and soul. We were as much married then as we ever would have been.'

'All right! All right!' Julia soothed, hands quickly gesturing appeasement. 'I was just stating a fact. Don't fly off the handle. I wasn't suggesting you were the least bit promiscuous. The point is, James is not going to understand why you'd quibble about going to bed with him. It might feel too soon to you, but obviously not to him. Why not go his way? Would it really hurt you, Suz? Wouldn't it help you to know if you can love him?'

Susan remained grimly silent. It seemed like a

betrayal to Kev to give herself to another man with less feeling. And yet . . . perhaps it was only a matter of time before that special certainty grew within her, and maybe that time would be accelerated if she shared that closest of all intimacies with James.

Julia sighed and fluttered her hands in protest at the long silence. 'Give it some thought anyway. James Kelleher is worth bending your personal rules a little for, don't you think? It's not as if you don't feel something pretty strong for him.'

'It was so . . . so physical,' Susan muttered lamely, feeling more confused than ever.

'Making love is physical,' Julia said drily. 'Don't knock it. If he's a good lover, that's one very big plus in a relationship.'

Susan shook her head, weary from the endless circle of her thoughts. 'I don't know. It doesn't seem enough somehow. Why can't he wait until I'm sure, Julia?'

The plaintive cry brought an ironic smile. 'I'd say he probably thinks it's the way to make sure of you. He wants you, Suz. That's not going to go away. You have to come to terms with it. Yes or no. If it were me, I'd grab him.'

'But it's me,' Susan murmured.

'And who's going to blame you for going to bed with him? Why make a big deal out of it? It's not a matter of life and death. If it turns out to be only physical pleasure, well what's wrong with that? And if you find it's more than just sex, then good luck to both of you. I'm telling you straight, Susan. You've got everything to gain and nothing to lose.'

Except my soul, Susan thought despondently, Julia meant well. She always meant well, but her advice scraped harshly over emotions which had been churning under more and more pressure as each day had passed. It was now Friday night and Monday was getting closer all the time. It was that deadline hammering relentlessly in Susan's brain which had prompted her to confide in her sister, but she wished now that Julia had not popped down to the flat for a sisterly chat.

'I don't want to talk about James any more, Julia,' she said tiredly. 'Would you mind going now? I feel worn out. It's been a long week.'

Julia reached across the table and patted her hand. 'All right, love. Enough said. Sleep on it.'

Sleep! If only she could! Hours later Susan was still lying in the darkness wide awake. Was Julia right? Her sister was so much older, more experienced, wiser to the ways of the world than Susan, yet Susan shied away from accepting her advice.

Somehow it was wrong. The situation was wrong. For the last three days James had been subtly laying claim to Susan; the intimate looks, so very personally for her, whenever he passed through the reception area, the delays with calls through the switchboard while he spoke to her, saying words which should have aroused pleasure but served instead to increase her tension. What to do? Was she crazy for hesitating?

At last sleep claimed her and it was a relief the next morning to wake up to Lindy's happy chatter and know that today could be spent in the innocent company of her daughter. It niggled Susan that James had dismissed the opportunity of meeting Lindy but she drove the thought out of her mind. She was not going to worry about James today. A much-needed respite was in order.

Shopping filled in the morning. Lindy's delight in being with her mother lifted Susan's spirits and she was easily persuaded into the idea of a picnic lunch in the park. To make the meal even more of a treat, they brought grapes and peaches and succumbed to the temptation of the cake shop, Lindy begging for her favourite fairy cakes.

'And one for Wally and one for Dave,' she urged, as Susan placed the order.

Susan smiled and increased the order. 'They may not be at the park, you know,' she warned her daughter.

'They'll come if we buy them fairy cakes,' Lindy reasoned.

'I hope so,' Susan sighed. She would welcome the distraction of Dave's conversation, and Wally was at least half the park's attraction for Lindy.

They were nowhere to be seen, however, when Susan and Lindy arrived for their picnic. Susan had not really expected them to be there at lunchtime and, while there was no certainty that they would appear later in the afternoon, she did not have the heart to dash Lindy's confidence in their eventual arrival. They set up their picnic under the shade of a tree. Lindy dutifully ate her sandwiches and was about to bite into a cake when Wally came tearing across the grass.

'See? I told you,' Lindy crowed triumphantly, her hand diving into the paper bag for another cake. 'Here's one for you, Wally. No, you can't have mine. Just sit down like a good boy and I'll feed you.'

Susan laughed at the motherly mimic in Lindy's voice, laughed even more at Wally's eager obedience, then lifted her gaze to the western entrance, expecting to see Dave strolling leisurely towards her. A man was approaching but surely it wasn't ... couldn't be Dave. But it was. Even from a distance his grin mocked her astonishment.

A smile grew inside her and beamed from her face. He looked like a new person, tidy, attractive, somehow younger and more vital. The curly hair had been cut and shaped to a fashionable length and the neatly trimmed beard leant his face a rather rakish but distinguished air. The red sports shirt was decidedly dashing teamed with dark blue jeans which were obviously new. Susan rose eagerly to greet him, her eyes shining happy approval.

'Dave, you look marvellous!'

'You mean I pass muster?'

'More than that! I could hardly believe my eyes. You've changed so much. You look ... oh, so much better. Tell me you feel better.'

He laughed. 'Maybe I do at that, if only for seeing the pleasure I've given you.' He dropped on to the grass near the picnic basket and stretched out indolently, propping himself up on one elbow and waving Susan to sit down. 'Go on with your lunch. Wally and I have eaten.'

'We bought you a cake,' Lindy informed him as she finished feeding Wally.

'Thanks, Lindy.' His eyes twinkled pleasure at Susan. 'You were expecting us?'

'More hope than expect. The park's not the same without you. I'm so pleased you came.'

Even his grin was somehow younger. 'Likewise. I would have been quite aggrieved at not being able to parade the results of your investment,' he said with an arch stroke of his newly cut beard.

'Worth every cent,' she declared and handed him a fairy cake. 'Here's your reward.'

He looked down at the pink icing with its thick coating of hundreds of calories and chuckled. 'Haven't had one of these since I was a kid.'

Wally waddled over, wagging his tail and

sniffing hopefully. 'You greedy dog! This is mine,' Dave told him sternly and disposed of the cake in one bite. 'Delicious!'

'They're my favourite,' Lindy said smugly, then screwed up her face in complaint. 'Why'd you cut your hair off, Dave? I won't be able to play horsies with you any more.'

'Course you can. I left the beard on purposely so it'll tickle your arms.'

Lindy giggled, shot to her feet, ran behind Dave and flung her arms around his neck.

'Whoa there! I might buck if you start strangling me,' Dave protested laughingly.

'It tickles.'

'Told you so.'

'I like you, Dave,' Lindy breathed contentedly, then giggled again. 'But I like Wally better. Come on, Wally. Let's run.'

They were off in a flash and Dave gave Susan a smile full of irony. 'The fickleness of women!'

'Rubbish! Lindy didn't change her mind. It was a matter of degree.'

His smile turned into a grimace. 'Beaten by a dog.'

Susan laughed and reached into the picnic basket. 'Want some grapes?'

'Are you going to pop them into my mouth?' He rolled on to his back, put his hands behind his head and opened his mouth invitingly.

'You'll catch a fly. I refuse to encourage your laziness, Dave Brown.'

'Laziness!' Instantly he was back up on his elbow, one eyebrow cocked in reproof. 'Here I am, all freshly barbered. Even ironed my shirt. What more does a man have to do?'

'Oh, you could get a job,' Susan said airily.

'Aha!' He held a finger aloft in smug triumph.

'I'm one step ahead of you. Now do I get the grapes?' His hand lowered, palm outwards.

She automatically dropped a bunch on to it while she stared at him in wide-eyed wonder. 'You've got a job?'

'Sure have.' He popped a grape into his mouth and held it between his teeth as he grinned at her.

She clapped her hands in delight. 'Oh, Dave! That's really marvellous. So that's why you could afford to buy new clothes.'

The grape disappeared and the grin became lopsided. 'I'm not short of money, Susan. Just decided it was time I looked presentable.'

She regretted the comment, realising it had hurt his pride. She covered her gaffe with a burst of enthusiasm for his job. 'You were so lucky to have found work so quickly. Do tell me all about it, Dave.'

He shrugged. 'I only signed up yesterday. Don't start 'til next week. Why don't you tell me about yours instead? Did you master the fiendish word-processor?'

'Not one mistake!' she declared proudly.

'Well, go on,' he urged. 'You've got five whole days to fill in for me.'

Five days. And only two more to go now. She did not want James to think she was playing a teasing game. She should have been more honest with him instead of using fear of pregnancy as an excuse. It had not been the whole truth. She wished he hadn't made such a strong sexual advance, wished she hadn't been so encouraging in her response. If only the attraction was deeper, based on far more understanding of each other. If only . . .

'Susan?'

Dave! She felt the tightness of strain in her face

and consciously relaxed, giving him an apologetic smile. 'Sorry! I was wool-gathering.'

'And not pleasantly.' The friendly hazel eyes were sharp with concern. 'Is the job causing you problems?'

'No. No problems at all,' she replied quickly. 'Everything's fine. I'm coping much better than I expected. It's a far more interesting place to work than Mr Everingham's office.' She flashed him a reassuring grin. 'The only problem is my feet. They want to wear sandals instead of high heels, and they sure let me know about it by the end of the day.'

The concern crinkled into amusement. 'I knew a doctor once. He had seven kids and wouldn't allow any of them to wear shoes. Insisted they go barefoot, even to church. Said shoes were an unhealthy abomination.'

'Well, I'm in total agreement with him,' Susan said feelingly.

All the same, if she had not taken off her shoes, and then her tights . . . Perhaps James had thought she was giving him a come-on after all. She shouldn't have let him play with her feet. Everything had happened so quickly after that. But the nonsense with her feet had seemed harmless. No. Not harmless. She could not deny the sensual thrill she had felt. And done nothing about. James did excite her. There was no doubt about that. He knew how to arouse . . .

The touch on her cheek was like James's light caress, and coming on top of her thoughts, Susan's instant reaction was a shuddering rejection. Her eyes flared fear at Dave before she realised it was he who had brushed her skin.

'Hey! I was only trying to draw your attention,' he explained, forehead puckering in puzzled thought. 'You haven't objected to my touching you before this.'

'I don't object. It wasn't you,' she answered hurriedly. 'It was ... I was thinking about something else and you startled me. That's all.'

'That something is very much on your mind. Twice you've drifted off into thought and I don't care for the look of tension you get on your face. So let's get the problem off your mind and out in the open. Maybe I can help.'

She sighed and shook her head. 'It's my problem, Dave. No one else can help.'

'Try me,' he insisted. 'You might be surprised.'

She evaded his too-perceptive gaze, drawing up her legs and resting her arms on her knees. 'It's too personal, Dave.'

'What you told me about Kev was very personal, Susan,' he reminded her softly. 'Aren't I friend enough to share your troubles?'

She threw him a rueful look but he was serious. Deadly serious. His face wore an expression which was oddly touching in its concern for her. She turned away, a prickle of tears blurring her eyes. Dave was her friend. Her only real friend in this vast city of Sydney. While she swallowed down the lump of emotion in her throat, Susan looked around the park for Lindy.

The little girl was trying to persuade Wally into sitting still at one end of the see-saw while she balanced herself on the other end. However, the moment the see-saw lifted, the dog forgot his instructions and leapt off, which necessitated a scolding and even firmer instructions from Lindy. Wally was being very good-natured about it all the Lindy was obviously enjoying bossing him around.

Susan drew in a deep breath and turned back to Dave, giving a wry little smile. 'Well, you did tell me to find myself a rich bloke,' she began, but the attempt at a joke fell very flat.

Dave did not smile. If anything his mouth tightened. The eyes which had invited her confidence were suddenly shuttered. He snapped off a blade of grass and began shredding it. 'And did you?' he asked tonelessly.

Susan hesitated, wondering if it was wiser not to tell him anything. But what did it matter? And maybe Dave could give her a man's viewpoint. 'I guess you could say he found me. To tell you the truth, I was amazed he asked me out.'

'You shouldn't have been. Your kind of beauty is quite rare,' came the dry comment.

'But he could have anyone, Dave. He's the most handsome man I've ever seen and he's got everything, not just looks. He's terribly intelligent, clever, good at all sport, successful in his career, charming, and he knows all the top people . . .'

'And who are the top people?' Dave interrupted in a sardonic drawl.

She made a grimace at him. 'You know what I mean. Celebrities and politicians and oh . . . the successful business people you hear about.'

'And how old is this paragon of men?'

'About your age. And it's funny you should call him that, because it's a good description, a paragon. And I'm . . . well, just me. It seemed incredible that he was really interested. It was so flattering, exhilarating. The first time he took me out we just talked, and, except for a very light, good night kiss, he didn't touch me. But the second time he took me to his place for the evening and . . .' A deep blush stained her cheeks. She was too embarrassed to look at Dave. 'Well, I got out of it that night but he wants me to go to bed with him. And next time . . . I've got 'til

Monday to decide. I do find him fascinating ...
exciting ... maybe ... '

'Don't!'

It was a command, sharp and strong. Susan
fluttered a look of surprise at him and found his
face grim, the hazel eyes dark with turbulent
emotion.

'You don't love him,' he said emphatically.

'No. At least, not like with Kev.' Her sigh was
heavy with remembrance. 'But, you see, maybe I
won't ever feel that way again. Julia says ... '

'To hell with what Julia says!' Dave burst out
angrily. 'That sister of yours judges on appearance,
and from what you've told me, this guy sweeps the
pool on appearances. Is that the worth of a man to
you?'

'No, you know it's not. Don't be angry with me,
Dave,' she pleaded, distressed by his reaction to
her confidence. 'You said you wanted to help me.'

He sighed and rubbed his eyes. 'I'm not angry
with you, Susan. I'm angry that you're being
pressured into such a position.' He dropped his
hand and looked at her with hard, searching eyes.
'What do you feel for me?'

The question startled her. Dave's tone of voice
carried an unusual intensity, almost an urgency.
She frowned, not understanding where the question
led. Dave knew she regarded him as a friend.

'You obviously aren't sure what you feel
towards your would-be seducer. I'm asking you if
you know what you feel towards me,' he persisted.

'Well, I've known you longer, Dave. I like you
very much. You know I do. I enjoy your company.
I care what happens to you ... ' She trailed off
uncertainly, wondering if she had answered him
enough.

'Would you go to bed with me?'

She stared at him in shock. Surely he couldn't be serious, but the hard, relentless look in his eyes were pinning her down. She hesitated far too long over a reply, not knowing how best to word a tactful negative.

'No. Of course you wouldn't,' he bit out harshly. 'You know me better. I think you even like me better than this man who's pressuring you. Yet of your own free will, you wouldn't choose to come to bed with me, would you?'

She had never thought of Dave in that way, didn't know how she'd react to a sexual approach from him. She suddenly felt frightened of their easy relationship changing. She liked it as it was. 'No,' she said decisively.

'Then don't be persuaded by appearances.' A grim look of determination settled on his face. 'I'll show you. I'll show you this very night. I'll take you to a party where all the so-called top people in Sydney will be gathered.'

'Oh, yes . . . where?' she said flippantly, sending him a dry look of disbelief.

He remained grim. 'I can arrange it.'

Susan laughed, hoping to jolly him out of his mood. 'Oh, come on, Dave. First of all you have to have an entrée into top society. You can't just barge into one of their parties uninvited. And another thing. You'd have to dress right to fit in. You and I simply don't belong, Dave. We'd stick out like sore thumbs.'

His mood had not lightened. It was even more brooding and his eyes kept boring relentlessly into hers. 'I'll hire you an evening gown if you don't have one.'

'Oh, don't be ridiculous,' she chided him.

'Do you have one or not?'

She shook her head in bewilderment. He seemed

set on a course which was impossible to accept. 'Yes, I have an evening dress, but Dave, please give this crazy idea up. I don't know anyone. You don't know anyone . . .'

His smile was grimly cynical. 'Oh, yes I do. I'll show you the very top of Sydney society. Wealth, power, success . . . all dressed up to dazzle and prove how wonderful they are. How very charming and intelligent and clever. The beautiful, glittering people. We'll see how impressed you are by the end of the evening when you've seen that your paragon is one of many with those attributes. All that is required of you is to dress in your very best and make some arrangement for Lindy to be looked after. I'll pick you up at eight o'clock tonight. Will your sister be at home?'

'Yes,' Susan answered dazedly. He spoke as if he really did know, yet how could he? Dave? An artist who hadn't even worked for some time?

'Will she oblige with Lindy or would you rather I hire a baby-sitter?' he bore on.

'No, Julia is very good with Lindy,' Susan said vaguely, still trying to come to terms with a totally unfamiliar Dave.

'I'm glad she's good at something,' came the acid retort.

Susan leapt instinctively to her sister's defence. 'Julia is very good at lots of things. And kind. And generous. You don't know her, Dave. Anything she's said . . . it's because she wants the best for me. She thinks of me as her kid sister who needs direction, and she's been right about a lot of things. So don't . . .'

'All right! I'm wrong! It will be my pleasure to meet your sister tonight. And your brother-in-law. Does that meet with your approval?'

'Yes. All right. It you want to,' she got out, still

in a daze. Why did everything seem to move too fast for her? A sense of unreality prompted her to ask again. 'Dave, do you really mean all this?'

'Without a doubt.' He climbed to his feet and looked down at her, a wry tenderness melting the hard cast from his face. 'I have to try to make you see, Susan. And now you'll have to excuse me. I have things to do before tonight.'

He strode off with more purpose in his gait than Susan had ever seen before. Not only his appearance had changed today, and Susan was totally bemused by the transformation. The lazy indifference was gone as if it had never been and, in its place, an inner power and a vehement passion had emanated from him with remarkable force. She couldn't even remember agreeing to go to this party with him but it was all arranged. And of course she would go. If for no other reason but curiosity.

Dave stopped by the sandpit to collect Wally and say goodbye to Lindy. He did not pause long and it was a disconsolate Lindy who trailed back to Susan and flopped down on the grass.

'Why did Dave have to go?' she demanded grumpily.

'He had things to do. And so have I. We'd better be getting home, Lindy.'

'Might as well now that Wally's gone,' came the resigned rejoinder.

However, once they were back in their own little flat, Lindy was quite content to settle down with the crayons and new colouring book they had bought that morning. Susan left her for a few minutes to slip upstairs to speak to Julia. She found her sister in the laundry ironing school shirts for the boys and Susan was able to put her request without wasting any time.

'Tonight!' Julia stopped ironing and frowned.

'Is it inconvenient?' Susan asked anxiously. 'Just say so, Julia. I know I've imposed on you this last week. I can . . .'

'No, no. It's no trouble. We're staying at home. It's just . . . well, I've been thinking.' She hesitated, clearly worried about something. Her eyes searched Susan's uncertainly. 'I might've given you the wrong advice last night. I wouldn't want you to go off and . . . and feel miserable afterwards. Do what you think is right, Suz.'

Susan's smile was wide with relief. 'Don't worry, Julia. I'm not going out with James tonight.'

'You're not? Then where?'

'I'm going to a party with Dave.'

The expressions which chased across Julia's face finally crystallised into frank disapproval. 'What are you thinking of? Going out with a hairy layabout! Honestly, Susan . . .'

Unwilling to listen to another tirade about Dave's unsuitability, Susan cut her sister short. 'He's my friend, Julia. He'll be here at eight o'clock tonight and please be nice to him. He wants to meet you and Brian. And if it makes you feel any better about it, he's had his hair trimmed and he's starting work next week. I'll bring Lindy up at seven-thirty to get her settled into bed before I go, if that's all right with you.'

'Fine!' The word was sharp with irritation. Julia picked up the iron again and thumped it down on a shirt. 'You are mad, Susan! Stark, raving mad! But I'll smile at your friend and take good care of Lindy. Just don't come to me when this Dave starts giving you problems. You've been warned.'

Susan gave her sister a hug and a quick, affectionate kiss on the cheek. 'Thanks. I don't

know what I'd do without you.' Then she skipped
out before Julia could start up again.

She hoped Dave did not have some grandiose
idea which would go horribly wrong. He probably
knew someone who knew someone who could get
them in to some high-class party, but she wished
he hadn't thought of it. If she was to wear evening
dress, he would probably have to hire a suit. Or
borrow one. And then transport would be a
problem. She should have said no. It was going to
be a lot of bother for Dave and for what purpose?

Because he was worried about her. Worried
enough to go to expense and trouble in order that
she might see more clearly what direction she
should take with James. Dear Dave. He really was
a very good friend to care so much about her.
Well, she would go to the trouble of looking her
very best for him, and whatever happened tonight,
she would be glad to have Dave at her side. An
amused grin spread across her face. It was lucky
she had persuaded him into a haircut or no one
would readily accept them as proper guests.

CHAPTER SEVEN

SUSAN worried over her reflection. The dark red taffeta was perfectly plain at the front, high-necked, demure little sleeves, a moulded bodice ending in a wide cummerbund which accentuated her small waist. Unpressed pleats lent some fullness to the skirt. The back view was quite dramatic, the plunging V of the neckline pointing to the huge, stiff, taffeta bow which finished the cummerbund.

Susan's cousin had chosen the style for her bridesmaids, figuring that the back view was more important than the front, where a bridesmaid carried a bouquet anyway. It was the only evening dress Susan owned. Since Kev's death she had had no occasion to buy anything formal and, but for her cousin's recent wedding, she would have had nothing at all suitable for a high-class party. She was not even sure that this was suitable, but it would have to do.

She wished she could have done something exciting with her hair, but at least it was clean and shiny and the gold slide-comb lent a little bit of glamour. She did not own any good jewellery so she wore none. With a careful hand she applied the matching dark red lipstick, then, last of all, slipped her feet into the high-heeled, black patent leather sandals which were murder to wear. Elegance certainly came at a price, she thought ruefully, and hoped there would be plenty of chairs wherever Dave was taking her.

'You look just like a princess, Mummy,' Lindy

declared with wide-eyed wonder. She had been watching television in the living-room and wandered into the bedroom just as Susan picked up her black beaded evening bag.

'Thank you, darling. Ready to go up to Aunty Julia now?'

Lindy gathered up Ragamuffin and Popsy, her two favourite dolls, and nodded her head. 'But you are going to tuck me in and tell me a story,' she said insistently, her big, dark eyes begging for reassurance.

Susan smiled all her love. 'Of course I am. Didn't I promise? Come on. I'll have time to tell you a long story.'

It was the third night in eight days that Susan would be leaving Lindy with Julia and, although tonight it was her daughter's bedtime, Susan realised that she was shaking Lindy's sense of security. She had been a stay-at-home mother since Lindy had been born and the recent changes in their life-style had to be a little unsettling. This starting a new life was fraught with more difficulties than she had imagined.

'Good Lord!' Julia's eyebrows disappeared under her fringe. 'You do look stunning, Suz, but aren't you a trifle overdressed for a party?'

'I don't really know. Dave said to wear my best evening dress, so I did.'

Julia rolled her eyes. 'He probably meant clean jeans and a spangled top.'

'Well, he can tell me if I'm all wrong,' Susan said quickly and ushered Lindy through the kitchen and into Derek's bedroom where there was a spare bed waiting for her.

'Didn't you say he was an artist?' Julia persisted, trailing after her.

'Yes.' Susan tucked Lindy in and smoothed her

hair away from her face. She flashed her sister a look of appeal. 'I promised Lindy a story.'

Julia raised her eyebrows again, shrugged and reluctantly withdrew. Wanting to avoid any further discussion of her outing with Dave, Susan deliberately spun the story out until the doorbell rang. She heard Brian's rather pompous voice intone a greeting as she kissed Lindy good night. By the time she had quietly closed the door on her daughter, no one was in the front hallway.

Assuming that Dave had been taken into the lounge Susan moved quickly, half-expecting him to be subjected to an uncomfortable quiz. Brian was not the most tactful of men and Julia's polite smile could freeze at ten paces. But the scene which met her eyes had her pausing in mid-step. Dave looked absolutely splendid in an immaculate evening suit, a suit moreover which fitted him to tailored perfection. He stood in the lounge with all the poise in the world, quite amazingly handsome, while Brian and Julia stared at him like stunned mullets.

For a moment Susan stared also, conscious of a curious tug at her heart. She tried to define its cause. Pride in her friend? No, it was a more personal feeling than that. Like . . . like she was glad this man was taking her out. Good Lord! Was she now attracted to Dave simply because he had donned an evening suit? She quickly shrugged off the feeling, berating herself for being affected by such a superficial change. All the same, there did seem to be a different air about him. He was speaking with casual confidence and was in total command of the situation as she stepped into the lounge.

'. . . last few years vegetating, but Susan has persuaded me to pick up my life again, so . . . ah, here she is!' His eyes sparkled over her. 'That deep red is perfect for you. Scarlett O'Hara come to life.'

Susan laughed, relieved that the dress was all right, delighted that his mood had lightened back to his usual, teasing manner and amused that Brian and Julia were so surprised by him. 'You look pretty smashing yourself, Dave.'

'One has to rise to the occasion,' he drawled mockingly, then smiled at Brian and Julia who were still remarkably silent. 'It's been a very great pleasure meeting you both. Susan's told me so much about you. But now, if you'll excuse us . . .'

Brian jerked as though a string had been pulled. 'Of course, of course,' he boomed magnanimously and almost rushed forward to see them to the door. 'Have yourself a good time, Susan. You too, Dave.' The words had the unctuous ring of a benediction.

Susan called good night to Julia, who hadn't moved at all. She raised her eyebrows at Dave as the door closed behind them. 'Well, you certainly made an impression. And where on earth did you get that lovely suit?'

He tucked her arm around his and smiled down at her. 'Oh, I dug it out of some mothballs.'

She laughed and shook her head at his nonsense. 'It looks as if it was made for you.'

'It was.'

She gave him a quizzical look but his bland expression seemed to confirm his assertion. Dave, owning an evening suit which had been made for him? He really must have dug it out of mothballs. Evening suits didn't date and in years gone by he must have had a reason to own one. It surprised her that he hadn't sold it.

Her attention was suddenly drawn to the car at the kerb. Its lines were very old-fashioned but the dark green paintwork gleamed as if the car was new. She did not recognise the model at all and when Dave held the passenger door open she could see that the interior was very old vintage, but in mint condition. The leather seat was soft and showed no wear at all and the dashboard looked like richly polished walnut. Susan sat and marvelled at the fittings while Dave took the seat behind the wheel.

'How did you get hold of this beautiful car? It must belong to a historic car club or something.'

He grinned at her. 'It does. It's a '53 Riley. RMF Series. Best one they ever made.'

'Don't tell me you stole it!'

'No, It's mine. I bought it a few years ago,' Dave said off-handedly. 'Most of the time it sits in the garage but I take it out for a run every now and again. It does handle beautifully.' With which comment he started the motor and proceeded to demonstrate how very well the car did handle.

Susan, however, did not relax and enjoy it. Every muscle was gradually tightening. Dave owned the car. On today's market such a car would fetch an enormous price, yet he had not sold it. He had kept it, along with his custom-made evening suit. He was far from down and out. Not even poor.

'What else have you been hiding from me?' she burst out, dark eyes challenging him with angry pride.

He glanced sharply at her, then countered her accusation with a soft answer. 'I never once pretended to be without means, Susan. You made assumptions which I corrected several times if you remember.'

'But you took the twenty dollars for the haircut.' The reminder was full of hurt. She remembered all right. Remembered his amusement over so many comments she had made. He could have been more forceful with the truth.

Dave sighed and gave her a look which was half-apology, half-appeal. 'Was that so reprehensible of me? You did press it on me, Susan, and in doing so, you showed you really cared about me. I felt so deeply touched. No one's ever given me so much. Not the money. It wasn't the money. It was a gesture from the heart and I valued it too much to knock it back.'

The hurt eased. While he had not been money-poor, there was no doubt in her mind that he had been poor as far as caring human contact was concerned. She sighed and sent him a wry little smile. 'Well, I guess I'll forgive you.'

His smile was warmly affectionate. 'Thank you. I might point out that I did carry out your wishes.'

She relaxed and grinned at him. 'You look so different. I bet you could make a few hearts flutter tonight if you wanted to.'

'Is yours fluttering?'

She laughed and shook her head, inwardly squirming over the initial flutter she had felt. 'I told you before. However you're dressed you're the same person to me.'

'I hope that's true, Susan,' he said quietly. 'I wouldn't like tonight to change anything between us.'

'How could it?'

He flicked her a sly look. 'Already you're seeing me as physically attractive to other women. Did you think that a week ago?'

'No,' she admitted. 'But be honest, Dave. You weren't exactly trying to be attractive.'

'The body's the same. Apart from the haircut, the only difference is clothes.'

'And they do make a difference,' she said drily.

'Yes, they do, don't they? I wonder if your paragon would look so attractive, stripped of his fine clothes and put in casual, old knockabouts. Would he be the same person to you?'

The question jolted her. She had almost forgotten James, yet Dave was taking her out tonight because of him, to prove something to her. The clothes were part of James's image. She simply couldn't imagine him in casual knockabouts. Even his shorts and sports shirt the other night had been well-cut and fashion-conscious. 'I don't know,' she murmured.

'Did you love Kev in any old clothes?'

'Oh yes,' she said with feeling.

Dave's ensuing silence emphasised the point. Susan was left with memories of Kev in the old grease-stained overalls he had used for working on his motor-bike, the torn jeans and T-shirt he had worn for lawn-mowing, the ragged shorts for swimming in the river. It was silly to envisage such things dimming her love for him. They were irrelevant.

'Where are we going?' she asked, realising that Dave had turned the car on to the approach for the Harbour Bridge.

'To Vaucluse.'

Even Susan knew that Vaucluse was the most exclusive suburb in Sydney, home for only the very wealthy. Her mind boggled for a moment. How could Dave known anyone in Vaucluse? Then she reminded herself that Dave was not a down-and-out artist. He owned this car, a vintage Riley.

'Just how well off are you?' she demanded abruptly.

'Well enough not to lack for anything I want. In a material sense. Money doesn't buy everything,' he added tonelessly.

Susan thought of Melanie. No amount of money could have saved his daughter's life, but Dave would have spent a great deal on trying. Maybe he did not have much now. Susan remembered him saying that his needs were small. Maybe the Riley was left over from more prosperous days, like his suit which had been dug out of mothballs. It hadn't been very tactful of her to bluntly ask how much he was worth.

'I'm sorry. It's none of my business,' she said just as abruptly.

Dave smiled at her. 'Well, I can afford to take you and Lindy to McDonald's whenever I like. Will you come again sometime?'

She grinned back at him, relieved that he hadn't taken offence. 'Love to. It was fun. I always enjoy being with you.'

'Susan . . .' The smile had flicked out. There was a sudden tension about him, an urgency in his eyes. He sighed and turned away.

'Yes?' she prompted curiously.

He did not reply.

'Dave? What were you going to say?'

'It'll keep to a better time,' he said off-handedly, not even glancing at her.

His withdrawal was disappointing. She had sensed he had been about to say something important. She shrugged away her curiosity and asked, 'Do you know many people who'll be at this party?'

'Quite a few.'

'Very well? Or just by sight?'

'Well enough. As well as I want to know them,' Dave commented cynically. 'Don't worry, Susan. We'll be readily accepted there, believe me.'

She supposed she had to believe him. He seemed confident that it would be so, but she certainly didn't understand how. She understood even less when he drove between the two massive stone pillars which supported the arch on which was carved the name, Kalianna.

The floodlit façade of the house confirmed that Susan had not been mistaken about the name. Kalianna was one of the most historic mansions in Sydney and was regularly featured in magazines. It was a mansion on the grand scale which required the services of a large staff from butler to under-gardener in order to keep it maintained in the style to which the Bartons had always been accustomed. A Barton had built it and a Barton still lived in it: Sir Geoffrey Barton, the media magnate, an awesome figure of wealth and power who wielded his influence with much-publicised arrogance.

Susan was struck dumb. A footman opened her door and helped her out of the car. Another took the car keys from Dave. The Riley was driven away. Dave took her elbow and steered her up the steps to a marble foyer where they were met by a silver-haired butler in tails.

'Good evening.' The greeting was given with royal dignity. It was followed by a respectful smile at Dave. 'May I say, sir, how very delighted we are that you're with us again. You've been sadly missed.'

'Thank you, Harrow. Very kind of you. But in a changing world, I suspect that only you are not expendable,' Dave answered smoothly.

The butler unbent enough to chuckle. 'Perhaps so, but institutions are not as amusing as those who tilt at them. Sir Geoffrey has been cock-a-hoop about your return.'

'Has he now? Well, you'd better lead us to him. This is Miss Susan Hardy, Harrow.'

'A pleasure to welcome you, miss.'

'Thank you,' Susan murmured weakly.

High society, Dave had said, and there was none higher in Sydney. And the butler addressing Dave as if he was a highly valued guest. She was stunned out of her mind and only the most disciplined concentration got her legs to walk as Harrow led the way to a huge reception room.

A glittering scene rushed in on her, dazing Susan even further. Crystal chandeliers, rich gold and white furnishings, people everywhere, the rich gowns and jewellery of the women shining out in sharp contrast to the black-suited men. The most immediate group was paying court to Sir Geoffrey Barton, immediately recognisable with his huge frame towering over everyone else, the thick iron-grey hair swept back like a mane and the short military moustache.

As soon as he glimpsed their appoach, the florid face, which had been frowning attentively to some-one's speech, suddenly sprang alive with delight. The group of people automatically parted, looking interestedly at the newcomers as Sir Geoffrey spread his arms wide and a huge grin split his face.

'Dave! I am so very pleased you changed your mind. I must assume I'm in this lady's debt for the pleasure of your company tonight.'

'You are,' Dave admitted candidly. 'Miss Susan Hardy, Sir Geoffrey Barton.'

Susan's hand was taken. Pale blue eyes twinkled open appreciation. 'My dear, I can well understand your persuading anyone to go anywhere,' Sir Geoffrey declared. 'You have my gratitude. Dave has shunned his public too long and we all look forward to having his pungent wit with us again.'

'All except the politicians,' an elderly gentleman put in drily. A hand was extended to Dave. 'But I'm more than happy to second Geoffrey's welcome back. My morning newspaper has not been the same without you, Dave. Always used to look at your page first.'

Someone laughed. 'I bet you did, Roly. To check if Dave was getting stuck into you.'

Laughter rippled around the group as Dave took the proferred hand and shook it. 'I always drew you with affection, Sir Roland. I'm sorry you have retired. Susan, Sir Roland Tate.'

'And I never once took offence, my boy. Your cartoons were always fair comment. A pleasure to meet you, my dear.'

He took Susan's hand and bowed with old-fashioned gallantry. Although Susan had no interest in politics, she knew that this man had been one of the longest-serving and most respected politicians in the country. She smiled and nodded, too flabbergasted to form words.

The puzzle was finally falling together. Dave's commercial work had been cartoons. Political cartoons. And apparently his work had been highly prized to earn so much respect from these people.

Another person pushed forward offering a handshake. 'Thought we'd lost you for good, Dave. Don't tell me you've spent all those millions you made.'

'Not quite . . .'

Millions! The introduction was completely lost on Susan this time. The face blurred in front of her and another took its place.

'Well, Dave, you're the living proof that the pen is mightier than the sword. Why is it, do you suppose, that Australians love to see their tall poppies cut down to size?'

'I don't think I do that, Walt. More like puncture them a little so they don't over-inflate their own importance.'

There was another burst of laughter.

'By God! It'll be great to have you in action again. Can't wait!'

A waiter arrived with a tray of drinks.

'I think we should toast the resurrection of Dave Brown, gentleman,' Sir Geoffrey said in the manner of a proclamation.

Everyone heartily agreed and helped themselves to a glass of champagne. Susan was handed one along with an indulgent smile. Sir Geoffrey's toast was amplified by a string of laudatory comments from everyone present.

Dave accepted them with a whimsical smile on his face. He met Susan's stunned gaze over the uplifted glasses and it dazed her even further to see tired cynicism in his eyes. He didn't care. He didn't care for any of this. It meant less than nothing to him that all these people respected and admired him. His expression changed to gentle mockery as he saw how deeply impressed she was by the accolades being showered upon him.

'Well, the first toast of many tonight, Geoff,' Sir Roland said with relish.

'Yes, this is a happy occasion, Roly. Very happy. Felicity couldn't be getting a finer man if I'd chosen him myself.'

'And didn't you?' the old man teased.

A sly smile lifted the military moustache. 'Perhaps I did promote the match a little. But Felicity's always been a headstrong girl. Would never be pushed into anything she didn't want.'

'I wonder who she gets that from,' was Sir Roland's sly retort.

Sir Geoffrey laughed and pride beamed from his eyes as he turned back to Dave. 'Now that you're here, Dave, you must meet my future son-in-law.'

Empty glasses were being returned to the tray

and Sir Geoffrey caught the waiter's attention. 'Tell my daughter and her fiancé that I have Dave Brown captured here and they're to come and pay their respects before he disappears again.'

'You'll be meeting the coming man in politics, Dave. Mark my words. He'll go far and quickly,' Sir Roland said with authority. 'Not only is he a very smart man, he is a very fine orator and he has that magic element, charisma. I haven't seen anyone like him since John F. Kennedy.'

'That's quite a name you're invoking there, Sir Roland,' Dave said sceptically.

'Believe me, I'm not exaggerating. He's prime minister material. The man has a remarkable record in every field, he has the kind of looks women swoon over, and if you thought Menzies and Whitlam were fine speakers, wait 'til you hear the voice of James Kelleher.'

James! No, it couldn't be! Not her James! Not engaged to be married to Felicity Barton. Susan's already dazed mind reeled against accepting it. James wouldn't have asked her out, let alone wanted to sleep with her if he was marrying someone else. It just couldn't be her James Kelleher. Yet Sir Roland's description was uncomfortably apt. There could hardly be two men of the same name with the same attributes. And James had said politics was his goal. But surely . . .

There he was. Dear God! He was weaving his way towards them, smiling his brilliant smile at people who called out to him as he passed, bending his head deferentially towards the stylish woman at his side whenever she spoke to him . . . so heartbreakingly handsome in formal clothes . . . and engaged to marry Felicity Barton!

His head lifted and for one electric moment

shock met shock as his gaze locked on to Susan's. His recovery was almost instant. No one but Susan would even have noticed the brief tightening of his face, the blank expression so swiftly corrected.

Someone from a nearby group hailed him and instead of continuing his approach he paused to exchange a few words. Felicity Barton tugged his arm, an obvious reminder that her father was waiting. The smile was back on James's face when he turned and his air of confidence firmly established.

One corner of Susan's brain marvelled at the control of the man even while the rest of her railed against his duplicity. Pride and an innate sense of dignity came to her aid. She would not be crushed by this humiliation. So James had played her for a fool while he had been already committed to Felicity Barton. Susan had Dave Brown at her side.

She slipped her arm through Dave's, linking him to her, not only for emotional support but as a retaliatory strike at James Kelleher. Susan herself might not be of any account, but it was to Dave Brown that Felicity Barton and James had been summoned, so Dave was the more important man.

CHAPTER EIGHT

'Ah, James,' Sir Geoffrey boomed. 'Come and meet the man who can help or hinder a political career.' He dropped his voice to deliver a jovial aside . . . 'I'd advise you to get on the right side of him,' . . . then lifted it to give his introduction a benevolent ring. 'Dave Brown, James Kelleher.'

The two men regarded each other speculatively for a moment, then with a disarming grin James thrust out his hand. 'How does it feel to be able to wield such power, Mr Brown?'

'Sir Geoffrey has been known to exaggerate,' Dave said drily, taking the proferred hand and idly shaking it. 'I am merely a commentator, Mr Kelleher.'

'One who can shape public opinion.'

Dave shrugged. 'The thought never crossed my mind. It simply amuses me to poke fun at the follies of people, and the most public follies are in politics.'

James chuckled appreciatively. 'Then when and if I commit a public folly, I can count on you to point out the error.'

'You're inviting me to?' Dave quizzed.

'I don't like making mistakes, Mr Brown, but I'd rather know about them so that they can be corrected. I don't propose to be a figure of ridicule if I can help it.'

'No. People of ambition usually find it difficult to laugh at themselves,' Dave remarked sardonically as he turned to Susan. 'May I introduce my . . .'

'No need ...' James cut in quickly. His smile invited Susan to share amusement but there was a wary reserve in his eyes. 'Miss Hardy is a much-valued member of the staff in our city office, and always a delight to see ... as she is tonight,' he added with charming emphasis.

Miss Hardy! So she was back to employee status in front of his fiancée. Two angry spots of colour burnt into Susan's cheeks but pride insisted she match his smile and tone. 'Thank you, Mr Kelleher.' Her gaze slid pointedly to the woman at his side whose bright blue eyes were regarding Susan with speculative interest. 'And may I congratulate you and Miss Barton on your engagement,' she added with sweet emphasis. 'It was a delight to see you walk down the room together. You look the perfect couple.'

Felicity Barton hugged James closer and laughed up at him. Not that she had far to laugh up. She was a tall woman, her long, silky hair more blonde than James', and she had the same polished, golden look which characterised James' appearance.

'Hear that, darling?' she purred. 'Wonder if we can live up to it.'

'Why not? The will to succeed is half the battle,' he said lightly.

'Well, Dave ...' Felicity sparkled with confidence, 'what do you think of my man?'

'Any man who takes you on, Felicity, would have to have more than the will to succeed. He'll need a will of iron to keep you in hand.'

'I wouldn't be marrying him if he didn't have that, Dave,' she said smugly. 'But James doesn't have to keep me in hand. This is one marriage which'll be a true partnership all the way.'

'And a very effective one I should think,' Dave

said slowly, his gaze shifting from Felicity to James. 'If you keep to it.'

The soft sting in those last words stabbed into Susan's heart. Had Dave guessed that James was the man who had pursued her? She hoped not. That would be too shaming to bear.

'You are a terrible old cynic, Dave Brown,' Felicity pouted, though her eyes still radiated confidence.

'Yes, I probably am, but it always gives me enormous pleasure to be proved wrong. You see, my dear Felicity, I'm a much disillusioned idealist. I really do wish you well and I hope, very sincerely, that you and your fiancé will be content with each other. And now, having given you my blessing, I hope you'll excuse us.'

He swept them all with a whimsical little smile and led Susan away before anyone could say a detaining word. Susan did not protest. She was beyond speech, seething with so many emotions that her mind was being bombarded with one wild thought after another.

Nothing was as it had seemed. Every word that James had ever spoken to her soured her memory. He had been committed elsewhere all right. Committed right down the line, and she writhed at the sheer gall of the man to have made a date with her on Monday night when this party was a public announcement of his engagement. How could he? How dared he?

'Would you like to go home?'

She looked up sharply. Dave's eyes were soft with compassion. He knew. No, no, he couldn't know. Not for certain. And pride insisted that he should not know. A wave of belligerence rose on the heels of pride. She was not going to run away from James, skulking off like a jilted woman. He deserved to worry over her presence here.

'Why should I? You wanted to show me high society so let's see all of it,' she threw at Dave defiantly. 'Who knows how much I'll learn? It's been very enlightening so far.'

He frowned, eyes narrowing on the feverish glitter in hers. 'I thought you might have seen enough.'

'Not at all. Lead on, Mr Brown. It's very flattering for a girl to have such a successful millionaire at her side,' she said with brittle gaiety.

His mouth twisted with cynicism. 'Becoming more attractive all the time, am I?'

'I'm waiting with bated breath for the next revelation,' she tossed off airily. Her feelings had been too lacerated for her to care what she said or how he read it.

Dave took her at her word. Face after face was introduced to her, some she recognised as celebrities, others just a blur of meaningless names since the social register had never had any interest for her. She smiled and clung to Dave, blindly sharing his identity amongst the whirl of prominent people about her.

After a while her mind was a merciful blank. The only thing impinging on it was a nagging message of pain from her cramped feet. She ignored it for some time but eventually decided that a respite in the powder room was more desirable than keeping up a façade of frivolity. Enough time had passed to have made her point if James had paid any attention to her progress around the party. Not once had she looked for him or shown any interest in his whereabouts.

Dave would have accompanied her out of the reception room but she firmly declined his offer, saying she would find her own way. One of the army of hovering waiters gave her directions which were easy to follow. She was almost at the door to the powder room when James caught up with her and, without a word, hustled her around a corner and into a dark room.

The door clicked shut and the light was switched on. They were in a library but Susan was not interested in her surroundings. She turned on James, flaring with anger.

'How dare you push me around! I have nothing to say to you, now or ever!'

He came at her, grim-faced with purpose. His hands gripped her upper arms while his eyes fiercely demanded her attention. 'What's Dave Brown to you, Susan?'

'Why should you care? It's none of your business!' she flung at him with all the fury of a woman scorned.

His fingers dug into her flesh and his face was taut with strain. 'Tell me!'

It was crazy but the thought flashed across Susan's mind that he was jealous. She shook her head, denying such insanity.

'Tell me!' he insisted, and the intense emotion darkening his eyes could not be denied.

'He's a friend.'

'You said you knew no one.'

Resentment flared. 'What right do you have to question me, James Kelleher?'

'The right of a man who thought you were someone very special, a woman he could trust. Is he your lover?'

'Trust!' she squeaked in outrage. 'And what about you? I thought you meant what you said to me.'

'I did. Every word,' he grated out vehemently.

'How could you? How could you?' she shrilled at him, hurt and humiliation bursting from her heart. 'Dave has been a good friend to me. A dear friend who brought me here tonight to show me high society because I was worried about getting out of my depth with you, James. I wanted to see your kind of world. And I did, didn't I?' she finished bitterly.

'Oh, God!' He closed his eyes and his jaw clenched as if in agony. 'I didn't plan for this to happen.' Each word was bitten off with angry frustration but when his eyes opened they were soft with pained apology. 'I'm sorry you were hurt, Susan. I meant to explain on Monday night.'

'Explain what?' Bewilderment took the sharp edge from her voice. 'That I'm all right to sleep with but you're marrying someone else?'

He shook his head in agonised denial. 'It's not like that.'

'No? Then tell me! Tell me what it's like,' she cried hysterically.

His hands whipped up to hold her face still, forcibly tilted to his. The vivid blue eyes were ablaze with passion. 'I love you. God knows I never expected to feel this way about a woman but I love you, Susan, and I have to have you, so please listen to me.'

It was true. The primitive, raw need of love was in his voice, his eyes, the hands cupping her face so possessively. The strength of his emotion curled around her heart, squeezing it until it thumped a wild protest at the violence being done to it.

'No,' she whispered in weak defence as he moved closer.

His hands slid down her throat, under her hair, fingers pressing urgency. 'I'm mad to be in here with you. See what you do to me. I should be out there working, cementing relationships, and all I've done tonight is watch you, waiting for an opportunity to get you alone. And each time you smiled at Dave Brown I could have killed you. I want your smiles. I want all of you to be mine. I need what only you can give me.'

With a groan torn out of the conflict of desires he crushed her against him, rocking her in a fierce embrace. Then his mouth was plundering hers, demanding her submission, and Susan's whole body quivered, vibrating with the force of his passion. But she too had suffered this night and rebellion screamed through her mind, insisting on rejection. She wrenched her mouth from his and beat her hands against his shoulders.

'No! Let me go! Let me go!' she panted, her breath coming in harsh sobs.

'Susan . . .'

The hoarse plea agitated her further. 'No! No!' Her voice found strength and rose in a wild crescendo of accusation. 'You're marrying Felicity Barton.'

His hold relaxed a little and she whirled away from him, almost tripping over in her haste to put distance between them. He reached out to steady her and she knocked his arm aside, instinctively leaving her own arm outstretched to ward him off as she backed away.

'This party was arranged, the marriage decided upon, before I even met you,' he hurled after her in emphatic defence.

'Then you shouldn't have asked me out . . . shouldn't have made love to me . . .' she countered fiercely.

'Do you think I don't know that?'

She reached a desk and moved behind it, frightened of the violent emotion on James's face.

He was working to get it under control and she stood there trembling, waiting, hoping that some sanity would prevail. His eyes kept devouring her with terrible intensity.

'That very first night I wanted you,' he stated flatly. 'But you seemed so innocent. Leave her alone, I said to myself. Say good night and forget this foolish attraction. But I'd already offered you transport during the train strike.'

His mouth curled with irony. No trouble, I said to myself. Until you got in my car and looked at me with those liquid dark eyes and I wanted you again. Innocent, I reminded myself. Leave her alone. But I found myself looking forward to the afternoon trip home, wanting to be with you, hungry for the warmth of your personality and the natural charm of your company. And I had to fight temptation all the way to Lane Cove.'

He thrust agitated fingers through his hair and shook his head. 'I couldn't believe it when your daughter ran out to you. It shattered the whole image of innocence I'd built to resist your attraction. At first I was shocked, but gradually shock turned into elation. I wouldn't be seducing an innocent if I took advantage of your attraction to me. And by that time I wanted you so damned much I figured that the only way to get you out of my head was to get you into bed and satisfy the nagging desire I felt.'

'You cold-bloodedly set out to get me into bed with you?' Susan choked out in horror.

'No!' One hand lifted in appeal, eyes anxiously denying the claim. 'It's what I told myself, Susan. What I reasoned out to justify . . . oh, bloody hell!' he breathed in disgust as he turned his back on the bitter condemnation glaring from her eyes.

He paced towards the door and for a moment

Susan thought he intended to leave. She was too churned up to feel relief. He stopped and wheeled around, gesturing a plea for belief.

'Nothing I've done with you was cold-blooded. I swear that's the truth, Susan. But you've got to understand. I didn't want to admit that what I felt for you was different. Oh, I said the words to you but I kept denying their truth in my mind, because I wouldn't consider anything interfering with my marriage to Felicity. That was fixed. Not only fixed, but precisely what I'd planned. I've lived for my ambition too long to throw it aside on a whim. Or a woman. No matter how appealing she was.'

He drew in a shuddering breath and sighed, releasing some of the tension from his body. 'So I took you home . . .' He started towards her, his voice dropping to a vibrant murmur, '. . . and I fell in love with you.'

'But you didn't break your engagement to Felicity,' Susan retorted, fighting the soft seduction of his voice and the warm caress of his eyes.

'No, I didn't. And I won't, Susan. What Felicity said tonight is correct. There's no love between us but what we do have is a partnership of like minds. We have the same goals and a very clear understanding of what has to be done to achieve them. It's a political marriage and to back out of it at this stage could be political suicide for me.'

Susan's chin shot up and her spine stiffened. 'That's that then, isn't it?'

'No. It needn't be.'

She eyed him warily, turning to fend him off as he walked around the desk. He lifted his hand to stroke her cheek and she flinched away from the contact.

'Don't do that! I don't want you to touch me,' she cried vehemently.

'Why? Because you know you'll respond?'

She shrank back a step, fearful that he still could arouse her if that was his intention.

He took her hands in his, fondling them gently as he spoke in his golden-honey voice. 'I do love you. I need you in my life, Susan. You're everything that I won't have with Felicity. You can have my apartment. I'll sign it over to you. I'll set up an independent income for you and Lindy. I'll see that you never want for anything. It'd be like a marriage, Susan.'

'No,' she whispered, aghast at the suggestion. Yet she was trembling again, shaken by the force of his desire for her.

'Yes.' It was a fiery hiss, sharp, insistent. He lifted her hands and placed the palms flat on his chest while his eyes held hers, hypnotic in their burning need. 'Feel my heart-beat. You're in my blood, Susan. You're the warmth I've always craved without realising what I was missing. To know you're there ... to be able to come to you ... I must have that much at least. I know such an arrangement won't satisfy either of us but you live with compromises all your life and it's the best compromise I can make.'

She said nothing. Her throat was completely dry, her tongue paralysed, but her eyes spoke rejection and he fought it determinedly.

'Is it such a terrible idea? Think, Susan. You have a child. You need someone to support you and you'll be able to give Lindy every advantage that wealth can provide. I'll take very good care of you, my love.'

The library door opened. There was no time for them to spring apart even if it had occurred to them to do so. The vibrant intimacy of the moment still bound them together. Only their heads moved, eyes instinctively drawn to the source of distraction.

CHAPTER NINE

IT was Dave. He took one sharp look at them, swiftly closed the door behind him and leaned against it, his face more grimly set than Susan had ever seen it.

'So this is why you wanted to stay,' he bit out with an edge of contempt which stung.

Guilt added its burden to Susan's confused state of mind. She had not meant to leave Dave for so long and the situation he had found her in looked entirely damning. 'Dave, please don't think I . . . I wanted this . . . this meeting,' she stammered on a plea for understanding.

'Oh, come on!' he cut back impatiently. 'You were using me out there to provoke Kelleher into it.'

'No! Truly I wasn't! I didn't mean to . . . to do anything.' The compelling need to keep Dave's good opinion forced the truth. 'I only stayed out of pride. I didn't expect this,' she confessed miserably.

His expression lost some of its hardness but his tone still had a biting edge. 'But you're still with him, despite the rotten deception he played on you. How can you let yourself listen to his sweet-talk?'

'You don't understand the situation, Brown,' James slid in smoothly. 'There's no call for your interference. If you'll . . .'

'No call!' Dave snarled in contempt. The look he gave James was pure venom. 'Save the diplomacy for those who can't stomach a fight,

Kelleher. I'm not one of them. Just spell out the play. Felicity is the main event and Susan on the side? The best of both worlds?'

'That's hardly your business, Brown,' James said coldly.

'I brought Susan here tonight. She's very much my business. And I take strong exception to a man who's so publicly engaged to another woman, sneaking my woman away to force his attentions on her.'

'Your woman!' James scoffed. 'If your pride's hurt, I apologise. But you know and I know you're nothing more than a friend to Susan.'

'And as her friend, I won't see her hurt by a self-serving bastard like you. Let go of Susan and back off, Kelleher. If ever a man deserved a punch in the nose, you do. And I'm itching to oblige, so don't press your luck.'

The clipped menace in Dave's voice sliced across the room. Susan sensed the tension in James's body as he gauged the seriousness of the challenge. And it was serious. Susan stared disbelievingly at Dave. He stood there projecting a power which could not be ignored, almost unrecognisable as the easy-going man from the park.

'Think how awkward it would be explaining a bloodied nose to the exalted company out there,' he continued with silky sarcasm. 'All those people you will have to impress. I don't give a damn what they think of me. I'm my own man. But you, Kelleher, you wouldn't look so good, would you?'

James sucked in a deep breath, lifted Susan's hands down and pressed them lightly before letting go. 'This will have to wait now, Susan. We'll talk on Monday. It'll be all right, I promise.' The soft assurance denied that Dave's threat had any effect on him and his eyes reassured her of love before he stepped back and swung to face Dave.

'Oh, no you don't, Kelleher.' No silk now. Dave's voice had the hard crack of a whip. He walked forward, a subtle arrogance in his lazy stride as he barred James's line to the door. 'You're not leaving this room just yet. We'll talk now. Not on Monday.'

Susan darted a nervous look at James, fearing a physical confrontation, but James made no move at all. Dave stopped some two metres short of him, hard purpose in every line of his stance.

'I have nothing to say to you, Brown.' The flat statement held a bite of resentment.

'Afraid that if you talk with me, the starry wool might be cleared from Susan's eyes?' Dave mocked.

It stung James into a terse reply. 'There is no wool. I've explained the situation to Susan and she understands. I don't have to explain anything to you.'

'No, you don't. I can read you like a book, and from my long experience of observing the political animal, I find the print large and clear. Does Susan understand you have no intention of breaking your engagement to Felicity Barton?'

James' mouth tightened for a moment, than spat defiance. 'Yes, she does.'

Dave shot Susan a hard, questioning look which made her shrink inside. She wished she had not listened to James or been swayed by his avowal of love. A sense of shame clutched her heart. By listening, by passively accepting, she was guilty of taking what James owed to the woman he had promised to marry.

'I see,' Dave grated out and looked his contempt at James. 'What line did you feed her? The king must marry a queen, even though he loves a commoner?'

An angry red crept up James's neck. 'I do love her, damn you!'

Dave's mouth curled in disgust. 'Don't disgrace your greed with the word, love, Kelleher. You lust after what she can give you, but the far greater lust is for power. Felicity Barton can give what's most important to you so you'll marry her. You don't love Susan. You want to use her, just as you use everyone to get what you want. You'd take her open-hearted innocence and squeeze it dry, giving nothing in return.'

'I'll give her a damned sight more than friendship!' James snarled. 'It's all so easy for you to moralise from the sidelines, isn't it? Dave Brown, the great commentator! But we're the ones living our lives and trying to make the most of them. You don't even know how to live. Take a long, hard look at yourself. What the hell have you accomplished in the last few years? Zero! So now you're ready for the come-back trail but there's no guarantee you'll be the success you were before. Maybe you've lost your touch, Brown. In any case, who are you to judge me? While you've been idling away your existence, I've given everything to succeed in whatever I do.'

'Given everything for your own glorification,' Dave commented acidly.

His face had tightened during James's long tirade. Susan had writhed at the unwitting callousness of the taunts which referred to the time Dave had been nursing his daughter. He had given everything to a person, not a career. She doubted that James would ever see that as a worthwhile occupation, but she did.

'I'll tell you what I've been doing, Kelleher.

Plumbing the depths you'll never reach because your capacity to feel for others is swallowed up by your immense ego. I haven't lost my touch, as you put it. What talent I have is based on a sharp perception of people and that has only grown and sharpened in the last few years. You have only a contempt for people.'

'That just shows how wrong you are,' James retorted scornfully. 'I love Susan and I'll provide her with everything she needs.'

'What? A house? Money? And a sneak visit from you when you can fit it into your schedule? Is that your idea of fulfilling all her needs, Kelleher?'

In an abrupt swing Dave turned to Susan, his eyes demanding that she listen and see. 'Do you really believe this man loves you, Susan? He won't give you his name. He'll never recognise you publicly. He won't be around enough to be a father to Lindy. I doubt that he'll ever show anything but a perfunctory interest in your daughter. He won't risk having children by you because that might prove awkward. He won't share your day-to-day joys or worries. He would have you live alone, cut off from the normal social life of couples, just so that when he wished to visit you, you'd be available to attend to his needs.'

It was a terrible life Dave drew, a life of closed-in loneliness which could not grow into anything else. Susan had not looked so far. The stark truth of Dave's word-picture was rammed home by James' casual dismissal of Lindy, of his pretence that Susan was merely an employee in front of the people who could help his ambition, and his repeated insistence of his needs, not hers. Never hers.

She looked at James in bewilderment. How could she have been so convinced that he loved

her? Had she simply been mesmerised by the
power of his voice and those expressive eyes? Both
those were the tools of an actor, a consummate
actor who could project whatever he wanted. He
did want her. She could not doubt that. There was
ample evidence of his desire for her. But love?

'Don't listen to him!' James burst out in furious
resentment. 'He's stressing negatives which will be
more than compensated for. We'll work it out on
Monday, Susan. You know how much I feel for
you. I wouldn't have risked staying in here if you
weren't so important to me.'

'You risked staying in here because you can't
bear to lose something you want,' Dave sliced
back at him before returning his gaze to Susan.
'You know why he wants to leave this discussion
until Monday night, don't you? So he can add
physical persuasion to whatever other inducements
he'll offer. He'll bed Felicity tonight and he'll bed
you on Monday night, and the only difference in
his sexual pleasure will be that he's having you for
the first time. Is that what you want, to be the
sweets on top of the meal Felicity provides? Is that
your idea of love?'

Susan felt sick. Her stomach churned with
revulsion.

'You bastard, Brown!' James seethed, then lost
his temper completely. 'You're not serving Susan's
interests in tearing me down. I'm the best damned
proposition she's ever likely to get. What prospect
has she got of marrying anyone who can give her
what I can? What prospect has she got of marrying
anyone at all, loaded down as she is with another
man's bastard child? You and your friendship!
You'd condemn her to a life of drudgery rather
than see her come to me, and what the hell good is
that!'

'You're wrong, Kelleher,' Dave stated quietly, his calm control a sharp contrast to James' wild fury. 'The very qualities which attracted you to Susan will attract other men, men who can offer her more than the half-life you'd give her.'

James' snort of amusement startled Susan. It signalled a complete change of mood. In an instant he had shrugged off his anger and in its place was a mixture of triumph and smug condescension.

'Men like you, Brown?' he taunted silkily. 'I'll have to concede that you're clever. You took me in with your spiel of righteous morality but I've got you taped now. The devious Sir Lancelot, come to protect virtue so he can take it himself.' He turned to Susan with arrogant assurance. 'He's not your friend. He's been arguing for his own interests, not yours. He wants to win your favour so he can get you into his bed.'

'It's a mistake to judge every man by yourself, Kelleher,' Dave said tersely.

James laughed. 'I'll let Susan do the judging.' The vivid blue eyes shone with compelling sincerity and his voice softened to a warm caress. 'I've been completely honest with you tonight, Susan. Brutally so, I know. But I don't want any more deception between us. I love you and I'll do all I can to look after you and your daughter. I wish I could stay with you now, but we'll talk on Monday.'

Susan shook her head from all the arguing and emotional turmoil. 'No. Please let it go, James. I don't want that sort of life.'

Urgency bit into his voice. 'Don't listen to Brown. I'll make it a good life for you, Susan. Remember how you felt with me the other night? You're very important to me. Necessary to me.'

'But not as necessary or as important as Felicity Barton,' Dave commented acidly.

James mouth tightened then curled with contempt as he turned to Dave. 'And speaking of other women, Felicity filled me in on yours, Brown. What happened to your last live-in companion? Before you feed Susan any more high-sounding drivel, why don't you let her judge the hypocrisy of the preacher? Tell her all about Jeannette Kray.' He shot one last, commanding look at Susan. 'We'll talk on Monday.' Then pointedly ignoring Dave he strode from the room.

Susan stared at the closed door, wishing she had given James a firmer rejection. His strong, vibrant personality seemed to drain her will and pull her towards him, yet she knew she could never accept the position of the other woman in his life. Even if James and Felicity were contracting a political marriage and there was no love between them, it was still a marriage she could not ignore.

'My God! Haven't you eyes to see? Ears to hear?'

The barely leashed anger in Dave's voice snapped her attention back to him. His face was white and strained, eyes stabbing with fierce emotion.

'The man has revealed himself for what he is! How can you still want him?' he hurled at her bitterly.

Susan was stunned for a moment. She had seen this anger directed at James but now it was aimed straight at her and its intensity was nerve-shaking. 'I ... I don't want him, Dave,' she denied defensively, apologetically, ashamed of the weakness James had evoked.

Dave expelled a frustrated breath and shook his head. 'Yes, you do, Susan. It was written on your face as Kelleher walked out.' The anger was more controlled, muted, but still there in the biting tone.

'No, Dave, truly,' she said earnestly. 'It's not what I want at all. I'll tell him so on Monday.'

'But you do want him even though you intend denying him.'

She was bewildered and distressed by this unexpected attack from Dave. She felt chastened enough by all that had happened and exhausted from the emotional tension James had generated. She couldn't cope with any more conflict. Her words were a tired plea for it to be over. 'I don't know what I feel about him and it doesn't matter any more. James has made his choice.'

'While ever he thinks you're vulnerable to persuasion he won't let you go,' Dave whipped back relentlessly. 'A man like Kelleher doesn't concede defeat until there's no chance left. Don't kid yourself that Monday will see the finish of it.'

'It has to be. It has to be,' she repeated on a wave of desperation.

Dave hesitated, his eyes probing hers keenly. Then in a hard, insistent voice, he asked, 'You really don't want any part of what he's offering?'

'No! I told you so. But when he's with me . . . when he kisses me . . .'

'For God's sake! Don't confuse sex with love. If that's all that's swaying you then I'll show you what it's worth right now.'

His approach held such an air of wild purpose that Susan suddenly felt frightened. This was not her dear, familiar Dave, but a volatile stranger, projecting violent emotion. She backed away, hands fluttering in fear, her eyes filling with tears of despair. It was all wrong. Everything was wrong. And this most wrong of all.

'Dave, please! Don't be so mad at me. I'm sorry I'm such a gullible fool, but I didn't mean to be.' The tears welled over and she covered her face with her hands as she sobbed, 'I didn't mean to be.'

Gentle arms enfolded her. 'Hush ... I'm the one who should be apologising.' The words were breathed on a soft sigh as he gathered her close and his embrace was a tender offering of comfort.

Relief eased away the jagged edges of tension and Susan sagged against him. He was her dear friend once more and it felt so good to lean on his strength, held safe within the circle of his undemanding arms. She rested her head on his shoulder and passively accepted the soothing stroke of his hand on her hair.

'Would you rather I hadn't interfered, Susan?' The low murmur was almost a rasp, tired, strained with doubt.

She sighed and closed her eyes. 'No. I needed you, Dave. I felt so confused.'

'And you don't any more?'

'Not about what I must do. You made me see how ugly it all is.'

His chest rose and fell heavily. 'Well, at least that much was achieved.'

'You're not still angry with me?'

'No. Please forgive that, Susan. I shouldn't have been angry with you at all. I doubt that even a much more experienced woman than you would have held out against Kelleher's talent for persuasion.'

The bitter irony in his voice discomfited Susan, even though the words denied any reproach for her weakness. The wish to escape from the whole wretched scene flooded through her. 'Can we go now, Dave? I don't think I can face that crowd again.'

'Yes, of course we'll go,' he assured her. 'But not home. You'll only brood over what's

happened here tonight. I want you to forget
Kelleher for a while.'

'How can I?' she muttered despondently.

'What you need is a pleasant distraction. I'll
take you to the best place in town. We'll order
ourselves a sumptuous supper, some good wine,
and we'll sit back and take in whatever entertainment is provided. How does that sound to
you?'

She pulled back enough to look up at him. 'It's
a kind thought, Dave, but I'm not really in the
mood to . . .'

He placed a hushing finger on her lips and soft
eyes begged her to reconsider. 'As a favour to me.
Let me try to put Kelleher out of your mind.
We've always enjoyed each other's company,
haven't we?'

She owed him that much. But for him she would
still be ignorant of James' intentions, and if
anyone could hold at bay the black depression
which threatened to roll over her, it was Dave. 'All
right. If you're sure you want to. But . . .'

'I want to.'

The warmth of his smile tugged at her heart and
a wave of gratitude brought tears to her eyes.
'Thanks for . . . for being here, Dave.'

The smile curled to one side. 'I brought you.
And the evening could hardly be counted a success
so far. The least I can do now is try to make some
amends. Come on. The world does not begin and
end with James Kelleher.'

She managed a watery smile. 'No, of course not.
Are you always right, Dave?'

'You know I'm not. But about this I am,' he
said confidently and tucked her arm around his.
'Are you ready to go?'

She nodded, surrendering herself to his keeping.

She wished she could always have someone like Dave to take care of her, someone good and wise and steady in this world of frightening uncertainties. It had always been a good feeling, being with him ... except for that highly charged moment in the library when ... she frowned, then shrugged off the disturbing memory. Dave was his old self again, her trusted friend.

CHAPTER TEN

THE butler jolted Susan out of her cosy frame of mind. Harrow's deferential response to Dave's request for the car to be brought around was a sharp reminder that the man at her side was no longer the man she had met in the park. Not only was Dave very wealthy and respected, but he had shed the passive indifference which had been stifling his vitality, and the man who had emerged was a very positive force indeed. He had been the equal of anyone at the party and more than a match for James during that awful scene in the library.

Susan began to wonder how well she really did know him. The thought gave her a strange, shifting feeling. Dave had lived a life she knew virtually nothing about. A life with Jeannette. She glanced curiously at him as they descended the front steps, seeing him for the first time as a man who had loved and been loved, a man who could command attention from any number of important people and yet one who was very much his own person, highly individual and very human. In fact, he was every bit as remarkable as James. Even more so since Dave's energies were not centred on self-advancement but on his concern for others.

Susan gave his arm an impulsive hug. He was a good person, a rare person, and she felt very lucky that he had given her his friendship.

Dave smiled down at her. 'Glad to be out of there?'

'And to be with you,' she replied artlessly.

148

The dark eyes scanned hers sharply before softening to a warm glow. 'I hope you keep thinking that, Susan.'

His hand slid over hers, enclosing it, squeezing gently. She instinctively returned the pressure, but what had seemed a mere gesture of affection and trust slowly changed texture. Susan grew increasingly conscious of strong fingers stroking hers. Dave had never held her hand before. This fondling somehow suggested a subtle change in their relationship and Susan wasn't sure how she felt about it. To withdraw from the contact would seem unfriendly and yet ... oh, maybe her nerve-endings were still jangling from the confrontation with James ... Dave's touch was not soothing. It insisted on a physical awareness which was disturbing.

The Riley stopped in front of them. Dave helped her into the passenger seat. Susan stared down at the hand he had released before closing the door on her. A confusion of thoughts ran through her mind. Dave was taking her to a nightclub. Like a date. Not like their meetings in the park at all. Had James been right? Was Dave interested in her as a woman? And if so, where would that lead? But Dave had denied James's assertion. Or had he? Oh, surely she was just being silly. Imagining things.

As he took the driver's seat Dave threw her a friendly grin which settled the matter. Of course she was being silly! Dave had no other intentions but his stated one, to give her some relief from the problem of James. But as they drove towards the city Susan's gaze was continually drawn to him, re-assessing the man in the light of tonight's events. He really was very attractive now that he had tidied himself up and obviously there was nothing he couldn't handle once he put his mind to it.

'If you keep looking at me like that, I shall start thinking I've turned into the son of Frankenstein,' Dave shot at her with twinkling amusement.

Susan gave a self-conscious laugh and shook her head. 'Well, you'll have to admit that you're not exactly the same man I gave money to for a haircut.'

'No, perhaps not,' he agreed with dry good humour. 'But then I hadn't found another mountain to climb.'

'Another mountain?'

'Well, I made it to the top the first time around. The view wasn't all it had promised to be. After a while I didn't even like it. And not even all the wealth I'd accrued could buy me what I most wanted. So I dropped off the top of the mountain. When you found me I guess I was just meandering in a valley and I had no reason to move out of it.'

Susan hesitated, then asked softly, 'Melanie was your daughter, wasn't she, Dave?'

He flicked her a look which held a shadow of the old pain, then returned his gaze to the road. 'Yes, she was mine. And I did live with Jeannette. But it was not the kind of hole-in-the-corner affair Kelleher was suggesting. I wanted marriage. She didn't. In any event, Jeannette and Melanie belong to the past now, just as Kev does, Susan. Whether you knew it or not, you held out a hand to me when you gave me that money. I suddenly saw the valley as a stagnant place and I wanted to follow you out of it.'

Susan's sigh was full of gratification. 'I'm glad I did that for you. I was hoping to give you a push and I was so thrilled today when you told me you'd got a job.' Dave's soft chuckle brought a wry smile to her lips. 'Not that you needed one. You really were very sneaky, not telling me you were rolling in money.'

'No. Money has nothing to do with it. You were right. Everyone needs an occupation. And talking of jobs, I'm going to need a secretary.' He flashed her a look which was both wary and too full of knowledge. 'You can start on Monday if you like.'

A job. Starting on Monday. So that she would not see James at all. Susan bit her lip and turned her face to the side-window, hiding a tumult of feeling. Dave was forcing the issue. If she had no intention of continuing in a relationship with James then this was an easy way out. Yet it was a way out which left her with little self-respect ... running to Dave for cover, taking advantage of his kindness and generosity because she was too weak to stand on her own two feet. Besides, she could not accept so much from him. No doubt millionaires could afford unnecessary secretaries but she did not want to be a kept woman. Not by James or Dave, however well-meaning the gesture.

'Do you want to keep working for Kelleher?'

The harshly grated question was edged with criticism and Susan reacted sharply, not pausing to think. 'Do you really need a secretary?'

Dave shot a startled look at her. 'You're thinking of me?' He gave a relieved little laugh and returned his attention to the road. 'I'm not offering charity, Susan. You wouldn't believe the amount of mail that will be rolling in by the end of the week. I used to have two secretaries working for me but I won't take on so much this time. It would be great to have you with me. We understand each other so well. In fact, I had it in mind to ask you this afternoon. But you were rather preoccupied.'

Her cheeks burnt with shame. It was bad enough that she had hopelessly misjudged James. Now she was getting Dave all wrong. The job was genuine. She should have realised that a successful cartoonist would attract a lot of mail. She just couldn't think straight tonight. There was no doubt it would be easier to put James out of her mind if she didn't have to see him day after day. And working for Dave would be a lot more pleasant than having Erica Ainsley's cold eyes shooting disapproval at her.

'All right,' she said decisively. 'You've got yourself a secretary. I'll resign from the law-office on Monday. And thank you very much, Dave. It's very kind of you to . . .'

'Not at all. I'm considering myself.' He flashed her a satisfied smile which settled the matter.

Susan breathed a sigh of relief. It was done. She had made a positive step. And it was right. She had to get out of James's sphere of influence and start afresh.

'Actually, you don't owe that office any loyalty, Susan. You could telephone in your resignation on Monday morning. They'll find a replacement fast enough.'

Susan squirmed. She knew Dave was advising her very tactfully not to meet James at all. Did he think she had so little backbone that she could not stand by her decision? It would be cowardly and inconsiderate not to turn up.

She did not imagine herself indispensable but it went against her nature to inconvenience people so selfishly. And to be completely honest with herself, Susan did not want to leave without seeing James one last time. It was most unlikely that he would change his mind about marrying Felicity Barton and Susan did not intend to become his mistress, but she needed a final resolution to their relationship.

'No, I've got to go there on Monday, Dave,' she said with quiet determination. 'I'll start with you on Tuesday, if that's all right.'

He did not like her answer. She could sense his disapproval in the short silence before he said, 'That'll be fine.'

His words carried a tight restraint. Susan began to worry if she was being foolish. Perhaps it would be wiser to keep out of James' way altogether. It was no use pretending that he did not have the power to influence her.

'You know, once you've become familiar with the job you could bring Lindy to work with you. I wouldn't mind her being there and she'll be happier with you than with her aunt.'

Dave's suggestion drove James out of Susan's mind. 'She'd love it! Oh Dave! That would be marvellous,' she spilled out with heartfelt gratitude. 'Are you sure she wouldn't be in the way?' she added, anxious not to presume too much on his generous nature.

He smiled away her anxiety. 'It's a big house with a safe play yard. Besides, I used to work with Melanie around me all the time. No problem.'

This time he said his daughter's name easily and Susan felt inordinately pleased that Dave really had shrugged off the past. 'Do you realise I don't even know where you live? As I recall, you avoided answering that question.'

He laughed. 'Maybe I didn't want to lose your sympathy. I'll show you tomorrow.'

Susan relaxed, content to leave the immediate future in Dave's hands. He really was the best friend anyone could possibly have. Without his positive actions she might have messed up her life.

It was his sharp perception and his forceful representation of what a future with James would mean that had saved her from folly tonight, and his job offer was an ideal solution to all her problems. Having such an attractive alternative to whatever James offered would surely give her the strength to stand firm against any persuasive tactics.

Dave had not been exaggerating when he had said he would take her to the best place in town. The Boulevard was one of the most expensive, most luxurious hotels in Sydney and one which frequently housed visiting celebrities. A smooth, silent lift whizzed them up to the twenty-fifth floor. Dave led her into a restaurant which was the very essence of luxury.

The room was at least two storeys high. From the tall, tall ceiling fell a mass of hanging baskets with a profusion of plants and ferns. Huge, crystal chandeliers lit their greenery and shed light on the scene below. In one corner a four-piece band provided music for dancers on the L-shaped floor which distanced the band from diners who preferred conversation. The blue-carpeted dining area was a few steps down from a glittering bar, and it spread to a wall of glass which laid bare the twinkling glow of the city far below.

'Do you have a fear of heights?' Dave asked as the head waiter approached them.

Susan shook her head. She was still drinking in the scene. Some of the women on the dance-floor wore the colourful way-out clothes which Susan had seen in shop windows and shrugged off as too fanciful to wear. She realised now that the city fashion scene had many sides which a country girl never saw. Well, she was seeing it all tonight, Susan mused, from the upper-class formality of

the Barton party to the international set at the
Boulevard. It was a long way from Lamamby.

The head waiter passed them to a lady who led
them to one of the window tables. Other waiters
descended on them with menus and wine lists.
Susan glanced at the lists and looked helplessly at
Dave. He ordered a bottle of champagne and a
seafood platter for two. Susan simply sat and
revelled in her surroundings.

Her gaze drifted to the fabulous view of the city,
the old suburb of Woolloomooloo immediately
below, the harbour, the north shore beyond,
stretching back into the distance. It was a strange
feeling being so high up, like sitting on top of the
world.

'What a fantastic place!' she whispered to Dave
as soon as they were left alone.

His smile held both pleasure and amusement at
her wide-eyed wonder. 'I'm glad you think so.'

She wrinkled her nose at him. 'I suppose you've
seen it all before.'

'Mmm. But not in your company. And that, my
sweet Susan, makes all the difference.'

The deliberate emphasis he gave the words and
the warm appreciation in Dave's eyes threw Susan
into confusion again. Every femine instinct told her
that the words and look did not belong to a
platonic friendship. Dave was projecting the kind
of interest a man shows to a woman and she was
reacting to it.

Her mind did not want to accept the reality of
the messages it was receiving. She needed Dave as
a friend. Needed to feel safe with him. He was her
anchor through stormy seas and if the basis of
their relationship was to change, she did not know
what she would do.

Dave's lips twisted into an ironic little smile.

'Don't look so alarmed. Is it so surprising that I should find you an attractive woman to be with?'

'You never have before,' she retorted, colouring with embarrassment at his accurate perception.

'On the contrary. I always have.' He leaned back in his chair and his eyes caressed her indulgently.

'But not . . .' Susan's cheeks grew hotter as she floundered. 'You know what I mean,' she accused weakly.

He grinned a wicked, teasing grin. 'But that was precisely how you were looking at me in the car when we left the Bartons.'

'That was only because you've changed so much tonight,' she argued.

'No. Your perception of me has changed. That's all. And the social restraints have been lifted.'

She frowned. 'What social restraints?'

'Up until you told me about Kev, I believed you were married. Up until tonight you believed I could hardly support myself, let alone anyone else. Both of us instinctively limited our relationship to friendship because within that framework we could enjoy each other's company with no hassles.'

'Can't we stay friends?' she pleaded, feeling her sense of security threatened and anxious to keep it from all risk.

He considered the fear and uncertainty in her eyes for a long moment before nodding. 'If that's what you want.'

Relief poured into her smile. 'I like what we have.'

His answering smile reassured her. 'So do I.'

A waiter appeared with the champagne. While he attended to their glasses Susan reflected on the relationship she and Dave had established. It was based on trust, a sharing of confidences, an ease of understanding, a genuine interest in and caring for each other. Having just experienced the emotional chaos of strong sexual attraction, Susan shied away from admitting to any physical attraction to Dave.

The waiter departed and Dave lifted his glass in a toast. 'To our working partnership.'

She relaxed and sipped her champagne. 'Hardly a partnership. You are the boss,' she reminded him.

His eyes twinkled pleasure at her. 'I prefer to think of us as a team.'

'What? You and me and Lindy and Wally,' she teased.

'Uh-huh. One big happy family.'

Susan was glad the seafood platter arrived at that moment. She was startled and highly disturbed by the inner leap of response she had felt at the idea of forming a happy family with Dave. Being with him all the time . . . Dave as a father to Lindy . . . as a loving husband.

She stared hard at the food and told herself she needed her head examined. All week she had churned over James. To suddenly switch to fantasising about Dave as a husband was shockingly fickle. Maybe the verbal duel between the two men had cast them as rivals in her muddled mind. She shook her head in a subconscious effort to clear her thought processes.

'Nothing there you like?'

She looked blankly at Dave before realising he was referring to the food. 'Oh yes! It all looks so attractive I hate to dig into it,' she said brightly.

'Well, I don't intend to sit here and admire it all night. I'm starving. Please do dig in.'

Lobster, crab-claws, oysters, prawns, scallops, caviar; the platter was absolutely laden with seafood delicacies, all artistically arranged on a bed of salad vegetables and accompanied by a selection of sauces to further tempt their appetite. Susan helped herself to a lavish meal. She was hungry and she decided that maybe a full stomach would settle her back to normal.

A roll of drums introduced the star female vocalist. She was a popular singer whom Susan had seen on televison variety shows. It was far more interesting to see her perform live. She belted out a string of songs with the punchy phrasing which characterised her style of singing. Her in-between patter was entertaining and the audience showed its appreciation with generous applause and much laughter.

Susan's enjoyment was heightened by having Dave to share it with her: the meeting of their eyes in mutual appreciation, the exchange of comments which expressed their similar reactions to the act, the whole sense of comfortable togetherness which stretched so easily between them.

The singer retired to a prolonged burst of applause. The band resumed their playing. Couples took to the dance-floor once more. Feeling replete from the delicious meal and pleasantly mellow from the wine, Susan readily accepted Dave's suggestion that they join them.

'I'll probably be as stiff as a board,' she warned him. 'I haven't danced for years.'

'Neither have I,' he smiled, 'but I daresay we'll manage a step or two together.'

Dave was a natural dancer, his whole body attuned to rhythm. As Susan gained in confidence he encouraged her to try more sophisticated movements and she found it an exciting challenge to match his every step. Finally she bungled an intricate move and he caught her in his arms as she was about to trip over her own feet.

She laughed up at him. 'I'm just not good enough for you.'

'Yes, you are. All you need is a little time to get used to me.'

The band switched to a slow tempo and Dave gathered her close, lightly pressing her body to his. A prickle of awareness ran over her skin as his hand spread across her bare back. She had leaned on Dave before; in the park when she had told him about Kev, and earlier tonight when James had left the library, but on neither occasion had the maleness of Dave's body impressed itself on her mind. Now, as they moved to the sensuous throb of the music, thigh brushing thigh, flesh pressing flesh, Susan could not think of anything else.

Panic raced around her veins, fighting the seductive power of sexual awareness. It was wrong to feel this way with Dave. He was her friend. She was going to work with him. She did not want sexual tension shadowing their relationship.

But how could she break away and insist on returning to their table? Dave would want to know why. He might be offended. He was not doing anything wrong. Just dancing. Susan concentrated on calming her pulse rate. She was simply being over-sensitive. Foolishly so. Dave was a man. She was a woman. This prolonged contact naturally aroused a physical awareness. It meant nothing more than that. Having argued away her panic, Susan relaxed and let herself enjoy the harmony of movement which Dave directed so smoothly.

He really was an expert dancer. After a while Susan felt perfectly content to float along with him. By the time the band played the last number for the night her hands were linked around Dave's waist and her head lay dreamily on his shoulder and nothing could have felt more right.

'Time to go home,' Dave murmured, brushing her ear with his lips.

Susan shivered with pleasure. 'Mmm. If you say so.'

His soft chuckle had a satisfied sound. 'You're almost asleep on your feet.'

'Mmm. Very tired,' she mumbled.

It had been a long night, emotionally and physically exhausting, and she did fall asleep on the way home. A gentle shake of her shoulder woke her up. Dave was at the passenger door, leaning across her to unclip her seat belt. He helped her out of the car and she sagged groggily against him as she stood. He supported her with one arm while he closed the door. She felt his chest expand and fall in a heavy sigh, then he was tilting her chin up.

'Susan, you must wake up properly. Where do I take you? To Julia's front door or to your flat?'

Her mind struggled to focus on his questions. 'Down the side path to my flat. It's at the back of the house.'

With a steadying arm around her waist he walked her down the path and around the house to the door of her flat. Still hugging her against him he found the key in her handbag and opened the door for her. Susan had left a lamp turned on in the living-room and even its dim light smarted her eyes for a moment. Dave removed the key from her door and placed it with her handbag on the kitchen counter.

She turned to him with a limp little smile. 'Thanks, Dave. Thanks for everything.'

On impulse she reached up to press a grateful kiss on his cheek but Dave checked the movement with a firm grip on her waist.

'Not like that, Susan. Like this.'

Before she grasped what was intended Dave was kissing her. Surprise caught her heart-beat and held it suspended until the sweet persuasion of soft lips set it hammering so wildly that Susan jerked her head back in alarm.

'What . . .' She gulped for breath and her eyes filled with questions. '. . . What are you doing?'

His smile was softly teasing. 'I thought you wanted to kiss me good night.'

'Yes, but . . .'

'Then you won't mind if I return the favour.'

He gave her no time to protest and once his mouth had reclaimed hers she no longer wanted to. It was a beautiful kiss, sensual enough to provoke a longer exploration yet not so demanding that she could think of withdrawing from it. Indeed, Susan was not thinking at all. She was engulfed in a tumult of feeling from which she had no wish to escape.

A joyous elation was singing through her veins and its song was one of belonging. The inhibitions which had been restraining her natural response to Dave melted away and she knew intuitively that this was where she wanted to be, in Dave's arms, being with him, of him, loving him. Her hands curled around his neck urging a deepening of the kiss.

He lifted his head for a moment, then plundered her mouth with a passion which carried all the need to possess. And she gave unreservedly. His hands slid down the curve of her spine and lower, thrusting her against him, and she exulted in the strong masculinity of his body, yielding her softness to it with all the long-awaited relief of a final surrender.

Having found her pliant to their touch Dave's

hands roamed upwards, over the roundness of her
hips, pausing to span the smallness of her waist,
then gliding up her ribcage to the underswell of
her breasts. His thumbs drew slow, tantalising
semi-circles of pleasure which awakened a melting
weakness for more.

Then abruptly his hands were removed as he
dragged his mouth from hers. He wrapped his
arms around her in a tight embrace and she felt
the almost imperceptible shudder which rippled
through him.

'Susan ...' Her name was a ragged breath,
whispering past her ear. She sensed the effort he
made to regain control before straightening up and
loosening his hold on her. She looked up at him
with eyes which still held the luminous sheen of
desire.

He sighed and stroked her cheek. He spoke in a
tone of wry tenderness. 'You are so damned
young and so very vulnerable and far, far too
innocent to be let loose unprotected. I did not
mean to go so far, Susan, and I hope you'll forgive
the advantage I took.'

She was about to say she did not mind at all but
he continued with barely a pause for breath. 'I set
out to manoeuvre you into a receptive mood,
dining, wining and dancing in a glamorous place. I
wanted to show you that any experienced man
could arouse a sexual awareness and draw a
response from you. I thought you should know
that before you meet up with Kelleher on Monday
because I'm damned sure you don't love him,
Susan. I didn't anticipate...'

He faltered, frowned, and for a moment a deep,
well of need darkened his eyes. 'You're a very
giving woman.' Then in a stronger, firmer voice,
he added, 'Don't be afraid that I'll ever encroach

on your generosity again. You can safely come and work with me and I'll be your friend, just as I've always been.'

Susan wanted to scream that she did not want that any more but she was so wretchedly confused by what he had said that she remained silent.

His smile seemed forced. 'I'll come around tomorrow and collect you and Lindy for lunch at my house. Then you'll know where to come on Tuesday. Good night, my dear, and thank you for ... thank you.'

He left before she could utter a word. Not that speech was possible anyhow. There was a huge lump of emotion choking her throat. And now the words could never be spoken.

CHAPTER ELEVEN

THE repetitive knocks on the door were sharp and insistent, beating through the heavy fog of sleep.

'Susan! It's almost eleven o'clock. Aren't you awake?'

Julia's impatient voice snapped the last barrier to full consciousness. Almost eleven o'clock. Dave would be coming soon. She needed time to compose herself for that meeting. Susan scrambled out of bed, darted over to the cupboard for her housecoat and hurried to answer her sister's summons, fixing a smile of greeting for Lindy on her face.

Her sister was alone. 'Thank Heaven!' Julia breathed and swept past Susan waving a newspaper. 'I thought you were dead to the world and this is no time to be dead to the world.' She slapped the newspaper down on the kitchen counter and stabbed at it with her finger. 'That two-timing wretch! You were there last night so you must know that James Kelleher is going to marry Felicity Barton.'

'Yes, I know.' Susan sighed and shut the door, wishing Julia had not read the social pages. She had no time for a prolonged discussion of James.

'It just makes my blood boil to think of what . . .' Julia's lips clamped into a thin line and she threw her hands up in disgust. 'I should've known it was too good to be true.'

Susan moved around her sister to get to the kitchen. 'It really doesn't matter, Julia. I didn't love him and I won't even be seeing him again

after Monday. I've decided to throw in my job.'
She filled the kettle and switched it on. 'Want
some coffee?'

Julia looked distracted. 'You know jobs aren't
easy to find, Suz. I understand how hurt you must
feel and I'd like to wring that . . .'

Susan quickly cut her off. 'I've got another job.
Dave needs a secretary and I'm going to work for
him.'

'Oh boy!' Julia breathed and shook her head
worriedly. 'You really do find them, don't you?
Honestly, Suz, you could have knocked me down
with a feather when he presented himself last night
as *the Dave Brown*. And taking you to a party
given by Sir Geoffrey Barton. Why didn't you tell
me?'

The hurt note in her voice and the reproach in
her eyes brought a helpless shrug from Susan. 'I'm
sorry, Julia, but I didn't know myself until after
I'd left the house. Dave hadn't talked about his
successful past and all I knew was that he taking
me to a party.'

'Humph! Then he's been deceiving you too.'

'Not really. We talked of other things. He's been
a good friend to me, Julia. A very good friend,' she
repeated dully, her heart aching from the necessity
of accepting that that was all he was ever likely to
be. The kettle boiled and Susan automatically
made coffee and passed a mug to Julia. 'In fact,
he'll be here any minute. Lindy and I are going to
his house for lunch, so if you'll excuse me, I must
wash and dress.'

'Suz . . .'

The anxious note in Julia's voice turned Susan
around from the bedroom doorway. Her sister's
forehead was creased with concern.

'. . . You don't think you might be jumping out

of the frying-pan and into the fire? I mean ...
well, Dave Brown is just about a superstar, Suz.
Even more out of your league than James
Kelleher. You don't think he might want to play
around? He did take you to a party last night.'

A wry smile curved Susan's mouth. 'It's not that
sort of relationship. You don't have to worry
about Dave. I'll come to no harm with him. He
would protect me ... even from myself.'

As Susan showered and dressed her mind dwelt
painfully on last night's stunning revelation of her
love for Dave. He had been intent on drawing a
sexual response from her and obviously he had
believed that was all she had given. But she knew
there had been a vast difference between the
mesmerising physical excitement James had raised
and the total surrender of herself she had offered
Dave.

He had been discomfited by the outcome of his
well meant manipulation. Susan suspected it had
been a long time since Dave had been with a
woman and his own sexual arousal had surprised
and embarrassed him just as much as the
unanticipated strength of her response. She
imagined that he would be at pains today to get
their relationship back on its old footing. There
was no doubt in her mind that he really did care
for her but he had stated all too plainly that she
was too young and too ignorant for him to be
harbouring an intimate interest in her.

And that was true, however much she wished
otherwise. Susan had to acknowledge that she was
too young and ignorant to be a match for Dave,
who was half her age again and whose wide
experience of life dwarfed her own small knowledge. While he was everything she could possibly
want, she fell hopelessly short of being able to

satisfy his sophisticated needs, and Dave had too much integrity to use her for sexual gratification, even if he was physically attracted to her.

She checked her appearance in the mirror. In T-shirt, jeans and sandals she looked exactly like a schoolgirl. With a hopeless little sigh Susan picked up her hairbrush and disciplined her hair to its usual neat shininess. She had to count herself fortunate that Dave had given her his friendship. Yesterday she had been content with that. She would just have to re-learn that contentment.

When she re-emerged from the bedroom she heard Julia's voice speaking outside the flat. Then Dave's. With a mental squaring of her shoulders Susan went out to greet him. Lindy saw her first. She glanced up from patting Wally and her eyes shone with excitement.

'Look, Mummy! Wally's come to play.'

'You see? I don't count at all,' Dave said in the amused drawl which was so characteristic of him. He was neatly and rather smartly dressed in cream jeans and a cream and white sports shirt, but even if he'd been wearing his sloppy old clothes it would have made no difference to Susan's feeling for him.

She did her best to smile naturally, hiding both the pleasure and pain of her new-found love. 'Sorry to keep you waiting. I'm afraid I overslept.'

'No hurry. I've been having a chat with Julia. I think I've just about succeeded in getting her to accept me as Dave Brown without the capital lettters.'

Julia gave a self-conscious laugh but it was plain to see that she was enormously pleased by Dave's casual friendliness. 'Go off with you now. I'll see you later, Suz.'

Dave made a business of handing the responsibility of holding Wally's leash to Lindy and the little girl's happy chatter served to cover the constraint Susan felt as they walked towards the park.

Dave seemed perfectly at ease. 'I thought we'd have a barbecue in my back yard. What do you say, Lindy? It's too beautiful a day to be indoors, don't you think?'

'I don't like barbecues unless I can have thin sausages,' she informed him.

'Plenty of thin sausages,' Dave promised.

'With tomato sauce.'

'I've got a big bottle handy.'

'Buns?' Lindy asked hopefully.

'Sorry. No buns. We'll have to make do with bread.'

'That's all right. I'll eat bread.'

'No cakes either, I'm afraid, but there's ice-cream in the freezer.'

'Does Wally like ice-cream?'

'He loves it. You'll have to watch out for yours or he'll sneak some.'

'He's a terribly greedy dog, isn't he, Dave?'

'I think all dogs are greedy. But you're right, Wally is terribly greedy.'

'You'd better watch out, Wally. You'll get too fat to run.'

The dog waddled along beside them, supremely content with his lot. Once they had reached the park, Lindy took him on a chase around the trees and Wally pranced around her, showing that he was not the least bit incapacitated by a weight problem.

'Are you upset with me, Susan?'

She glanced sharply at Dave, saw the deep concern in his eyes and quickly dropped her lashes. 'No. No, of course not.' The inevitable rush of heat to her cheeks made her feel even more self-conscious. 'I'm very grateful for all you did for me last night.'

He did not speak for several long moments and Susan could not look at him for fear of revealing the torment of her unrequited love.

'I thought you might have felt I'd abused your trust.'

She shook her head. 'When Julia was suspicious of you a couple of weeks ago I told her I'd trust you with my life. It was true then and it's even more true now. I know you wouldn't do anything you thought wasn't good for me.'

'Susan, I'm a man. Not a saint. My judgments and actions are not always without self-interest. I'm as much motivated by what I want as the next man.'

The strained note in his voice and the terse emphasis with which he had delivered the words gave Susan pause for thought. A little hope crawled into her heart. Was it possible that Dave had more than a benevolent interest in her? She slanted a cautious look of enquiry at him.

'What did you get out of last night?'

His lips slowly twitched into a dry little smile. 'I got myself a secretary.'

'So you did,' she agreed flatly. 'But I rather fancy that's more to my advantage than yours.'

His grin drove out the last feeble tentacles of hope. 'Don't you believe it! It's extremely difficult to find someone with whom one can communicate without irritation.'

'Well, I'll try very hard not to get in your hair.'

'What there is left of it,' he mocked, running his fingers through his shorn locks and teasing a smile out of her. Then apparently satisfied that any disturbing ripple in their friendship had been smoothed out, he called Lindy and Wally to join them and they strolled on.

Dave's home was a two-storey house which stood directly opposite the western entrance of the park. It was built in the conventional style of some forty years ago, solid red brick with a white-pillared portico and a balcony above it. The front garden was very small, a narrow strip of lawn each side of the path and old camellia bushes crowding up against the wall of the house.

The stained glass panels of the front door and two sidelights threw a pleasantly muted light into the spacious hallway. They passed by a dining-room and living-room and Susan could not help comparing the comfortable, rather old-fashioned furnishings to the sleek modernity of James's apartment. Here there was no concern about images. The house was for living in.

Dave ushered them into a bright, cheerful kitchen which opened on to an equally attractive breakfast room. Glass doors led out to a patio and barbecue area which was shaded by a vine-covered pergola, and beyond this was a good-sized garden, high-fenced for complete privacy and containing well-established trees and shrubs.

'The fence is dog-and-child-proof.' Dave commented as he invited them outside. 'Lindy will be perfectly safe playing out here with Wally.'

Lindy was already off and exploring with an excited dog at her heels. Susan watched her indulgently. 'It's a lovely area, Dave. I wonder that you ever bothered going over to the park.'

'One gets tired of one's own company,' he said drily. 'The park's more sociable. You meet all sort of people there.'

Susan smiled. 'I guess you do. Even famous cartoonists.'

He laughed and waved an invitation to the redwood furniture which was handily placed near the barbecue. 'Sit down and relax. I'll show you my workroom after lunch. Meanwhile, if you'll excuse me a minute, I'll raid the refrigerator for thin sausages.'

It was a very informal lunch. Dave cooked sausages, steaks, potato chips and onions on the barbecue. He brought out bread and cheese and a big bowl of salad and they all helped themselves to whatever they wanted. Wally made short work of the leftovers. Ice-cream was duly served. Lindy was clearly delighted with everything and during lunch she positively basked in Dave's kindly attention. He really had a wonderful way with children and Susan ruefully thought that he probably considered her little more than a child, too.

When Lindy began to wilt from all the excitement Dave suggested she might like to see a video of *The Wizard of Oz*. In no time at all he had her happily settled in the lounge, the dog nestled beside her and Judy Garland's immortal Dorothy playing out her adventures on the television screen. Lindy merely nodded uninterestedly when Dave told her he was taking her mother upstairs to show her his work.

The staircase was in the hallway, just outside the lounge, so Lindy could easily find them, but it was obvious that the little girl was content to stay where she was. As Susan accompanied Dave upstairs she felt assured that Lindy would cause no problem to Dave if she came here during work hours.

The only real problem was going to be herself, and her awareness of that problem mounted inexorably as the afternoon wore on. Dave showed her the originals of his most successful cartoons, books which featured annual collections of his work and personality calendars which he had marketed. Her ignorance of the political world lessened her appreciation of the pertinence in the cartoons but the cleverness of the sketches and the wit and wisdom of Dave Brown were very evident. The more Dave showed of himself the more deeply she loved him and the more inadequate she felt herself.

She used the excuse of checking on Lindy to take a breathing space away from him. The emotion she was trying to contain was choking her. Lindy was blissfully asleep. Wally gave a low growl and watched Susan with suspicious eyes as she pushed a cushion under her daughter's head. The dog was as protective as its master. Susan fiercely wished that Dave could feel more than protective towards her but a sense of utter hopelessness dragged her feet as she trudged back upstairs.

Dave had left the desk and was standing at one of the windows. His work-room was a combination of a study and an artist's studio and the eastern and northern walls had large windows. He made no move and her gaze followed his as she joined him.

'You can see our park bench,' she said in surprise.

'Yes. I saw you and Lindy arrive for your picnic yesterday and decided to crash in on it.' He sighed and turned to her with a wry smile. 'Just as well I did or I wouldn't have known about Kelleher. How do you feel about tomorrow, Susan?'

The blunt question wrecked her careful composure. She did not want to be reminded of what a fool she'd been. 'I don't know. I'll find out when I get to the office I suppose,' she muttered dispiritedly.

Dave's eyes burnt into hers, intensely demanding. 'You won't let him change your mind?'

She turned her head away, miserable at the thought that Dave imagined her to be still infatuated with James. 'I won't change my mind,' she echoed dully.

Dave heaved another sigh. 'I'm sorry. Stupid of me to bring it up. Come and I'll show you the cartoons of Wally I used to draw for Melanie. I've been thinking of using them for a children's book. Maybe you can suggest a story that'd make sense of them.'

The sketches of Wally were superb, capturing his playful antics and giving him all the doggy variations of human expression. Dave threw around several possible story-lines and Susan elaborated on them with ideas of her own. It made her feel useful and the project was so interesting and stimulating that she forgot all about her heartache. She and Dave were still re-arranging sequences of sketches when Lindy and Wally came trundling into the room, and then Lindy was so entranced with the pictures that she had to see every one of them.

Eventually Dave insisted on their having afternoon tea. By the time this was finished Susan was startled to find it was almost five o'clock. Dave brushed aside her apologies for staying so late and would not hear of letting them walk home alone. He and Wally accompanied them all the way and Susan could not help fantasising that they were a family group on a Sunday afternoon stroll.

'Bring Lindy on Tuesday if you like. She'll be no trouble,' Dave assured her as they prepared to part at Julia's front gate.

'Thanks, Dave. And thanks for today too. We had a lovely time.'

'My pleasure,' he smiled, but the smile abruptly faded, replaced by a taut look of concern. 'Susan, you really don't have to go in to the office tomorrow. Kelleher doesn't deserve any consideration from you.'

She heaved a sigh of frustration. Why did he have to bring up James again? She wished he had left her with the smile. 'Dave, I can't leave it the way it is. I have to see James again,' she said tersely.

He frowned. 'Susan, I . . .'

'Oh, please drop it!' The anguish in her voice silenced him but the pained look on Dave's face made Susan instantly contrite. 'I'm sorry, but I have to do what I think best.'

Her apology seemed to have the effect of a slap. His expression took on a bleak, withdrawn air. 'Tuesday then,' he muttered and strode briskly away.

Susan bit her lips in vexation. She should not have lashed out at Dave like that. He had meant well. Oh, damn it all! Couldn't he see that she was not a child who had to be protected all the time? She was a woman. A fully grown woman who desperately wanted his love and respect.

With a moan of despair Susan swung an unusually silent Lindy up into her arms and hugged her close, wishing with all her heart that Dave could belong to both of them. He did care about them, a little hope whispered, and maybe it wasn't impossible that he should come to love them if they were with him constantly. It wasn't impossible, she insisted to herself as she walked down to the flat to get ready for tomorrow.

CHAPTER TWELVE

'Hi, Susan! Have a good weekend?'

Denise Rowe's cheery greeting fell like a lead balloon on the nervous butterflies in Susan's stomach. They were squashed, along with the hope she had nursed of sneaking a private meeting with James.

'Not bad. And you?' she replied automatically.

Denise rattled out a brief account of her doings which Susan barely heard. Fate was definitely against her. Two buses had passed her by this morning, already loaded with passengers. The one which finally picked her up had crawled into the city. Even though she had still arrived ten minutes earlier than usual, Denise's presence behind the reception desk complicated her plan to get the talk with James over with as soon as possible.

Feeling very disgruntled Susan settled herself at the switchboard. Having keyed herself up to confront James with a determined rejection first thing this morning she did not know what to do now. She really wanted to have that scene over with before handing her resignation to Erica Ainsley.

A buzz from the switchboard drew her attention. Susan's pulse leapt as she saw it was from James's office. Maybe it was still possible to see him. She swiftly connected the line to hers.

'Good morning, Mr Kelleher.'

'Susan?' The golden-honey voice held an urgent note.

Susan's heart cringed in anticipation of its persuasive appeal. 'Yes sir?' she said nervously.

'Is Denise there?'

'Yes sir.'

'Tell her to look after the switchboard. I want to see you in my office. At once.'

The peremptory summons and the swift click of disconnection allowed no argument. Susan slowly removed the headphone, aware of tension creeping through her body. The confrontation which she had mentally postponed was upon her now. Whatever James' motive was for ignoring the discretion he himself had emphasised, Susan had to take this opportunity to end their relationship.

James' instructions brought an arch look from Denise but Susan ignored the girl's curiosity. She had more pressing matters to think about on the short walk to James' office. While she was relieved that she would not have to wait all day before seeing him, his urgency to see her was disturbing. Could he love her so much that he no longer cared who knew it? Had he broken with Felicity Barton? Surely he would not have risked his political future for love of her.

Susan took a deep, determined breath as she opened his door. It had to be a quick, clean break. She did not love James and she was not going to be swayed by anything he said or did.

He gave her no time to say anything. The moment she entered James was pushing the door shut and pulling her into his arms. 'I couldn't wait. I know this is insane but I couldn't wait another minute.'

He held her so tightly Susan could scarcely breathe, but the flutter in her heart had nothing to do with love or physical excitement. It was nervous fear. Already this meeting seemed out of her control. James was brushing his lips across her hair as he continued muttering with passionate longing.

'I thought yesterday would never come to an end. My God! I need you, Susan. I feel starved for your sweet simplicity and honest emotion after the farce I've acted out this weekend. Say you need me.'

He drew back enough to look down at her and the vivid blue eyes blazed with desire. Susan gulped and opened her mouth to deny his entreaty but before she could utter a word he was kissing her, ravishing her mouth with his own. The sheer passion of his invasion shocked her into passivity for a moment. Then resentment boiled to the fore and she pushed at him with all her strength.

'No! I don't need you. I don't love you. I don't want you,' she gabbled, as she forced him away.

He caught her upper arms and his fingers dug insistently into the soft flesh. 'Susan! What's got into you? How can you say that?' Then in quick response to the stubborn set of her face, his voice dropped to a persuasive purr. 'Remember last Tuesday night? We felt the same need. The same desire. You can't lie to me or yourself about that, Susan. You love me.'

'No!' she cried with all the bitterness of shame. 'I'm not used to being . . . being touched like that. Not even kissed like that. I haven't been with a man . . . not even on a date since before Lindy was born. But it wasn't love. It was a physical thing. And it frightened me. That's why I told Dave about it.'

'Brown!' His teeth clenched on the name. 'He's behind this change of mind, isn't he? You've been listening to him.'

'Yes. Yes, I have,' Susan threw back defiantly.

'Don't you realise he wants you for himself?'

'No, he doesn't. But I wish he did. I wish he did,' she repeated vehemently, angry that James was dismissing everything she'd said.

His reaction frightened her. Blue fire stabbed from his eyes, cruel, dangerous and determined. 'He's not going to have you. You're mine and you'll stay mine.'

It suddenly burst on Susan that love or the loss of it had nothing to do with his claim. This was the sheer hatred of being beaten. It was as Dave said. James Kelleher would not accept defeat.

'I do have some say in that, James,' she said with a determination that equalled his. 'I don't want you in my life and from now on I want you to leave me alone. You've made a commitment to Felicity Barton and I think you should honour it.'

Immediately his expression softened to one of appeasement. 'So, it's Felicity you're worrying about.' His hands loosened their grip and began to rub her arms in a sensual caress. 'Susan, she's like a business partner. Our marriage will be a contract of convenience, nothing that will impinge on what we have together.'

Susan stepped back out of his grasp. 'We're not going to have anything together. I mean that, James.'

'No, you don't. You can't.' He was reaching for her again when the telephone rang. He swore under his breath, seemed about to ignore the summons, then snatched up Susan's hand and pulled her with him to the desk. His eyes commanded her silent acquiescence as he lifted the receiver. 'James Kelleher,' he announced curtly.

Susan eyed him resentfully, her vision unclouded by any confused emotions. No longer was she overwhelmed by his golden looks and charm. The shining charisma which marked him as the winner he had always been had lost its power to win her to his side. Compared to Dave, James was just a glamorous shell and if he had a heart at all, it beat only for James Kelleher.

'I told you not to call me here.' Irritation soured the honey voice and thinned his lips as he listened to the voice on the other end of the line. The communication was obviously unwelcome. 'Goddammit, Felicity! I'm busy! You'll have to handle it yourself.'

Anger seethed over Susan's resentment. The hypocrisy of the man! How dared he stand there holding her hand while he spoke to his fiancée!

The blue eyes flashed to her, burning with an intensity which brooked no denial. 'No. I have an important meeting tonight. Use your own judgment. I'll go along with whatever you decide.' He hung up and reached for Susan's other hand.

She whipped it behind her back and flung her anger at him. 'Let me go, James, or I'll scream this office down. And that wouldn't be at all discreet, would it?'

'Susan! For God's sake! Can't you see I'm putting you ahead of Felicity?' he said impatiently.

'Just put me out of your life altogether. I don't want to argue. There's nothing to argue about. It's finished so let me go.'

'No!'

He jerked her towards him. Tipped off-balance Susan brought her free hand up to slam against his chest. Instantly James covered it with his, imprisoning it there as his head bent to hers.

The door opened. Susan's disbelieving eyes registered the taut figure of Dave Brown but her brain refused to accept the physical reality. Time seemed to shift backwards, repeating the moment when he had stepped into the Barton library on Saturday night. She and James were standing in virtually the same pose, Dave's face wore the same grim expression, and the same tension whipped across the room.

Only when Dave shut the door did Susan's mind click into feverish activity. She did not understand what he was doing here in James's office but an anxious well of emotion insisted that he be assured that this scene was different.

'Dave, no! It's not . . .'

Her protest was cut off by a bristling James. 'What the hell do you think you're doing here, Brown?'

'Taking up where I left off on Saturday night,' came the equally belligerent answer.

'Get out of my office!' James snarled.

'Not without Susan,' Dave snapped back at him.

'Stop it! Just stop it!' Susan cried in frustration. 'Will you please listen to me!'

'Not until I've said what I've come to say,' Dave retorted fiercely.

She tried again. 'It's not what you . . .'

'Susan! Just hear me out!'

'Just hear him out,' James mocked viciously, squeezing Susan's hands to regain her attention. 'And this is the man you say doesn't want you. He's no better than . . .'

'Yes, I want her!'

The blunt declaration was flung across the room, silencing James and drawing Susan's stunned gaze.

Dave's eyes bored into hers. 'Whatever he's offered you, Susan, you know I can offer more. I'll always be at hand to look after you and give you the companionship he'll never give you. I'll be a caring father to Lindy and any other children you'd like to have ...'

'Oh, that's all very fine, Brown!' James scoffed. 'But you don't turn Susan on. I'm the man she wants.'

Dave ignored him, his gaze not wavering one iota from Susan's. 'You didn't push me away on Saturday night. You feel something for me, Susan. Isn't it enough when you balance out the rest? Wouldn't you rather be my wife than his part time mistress?'

'Your wife?' Her mouth could hardly form the words.

'He's lying! He'll never marry you.'

Her ears vaguely heard James' assertions but they were dim sounds against the thunderous beat of her heart which kept drumming out the echo of Dave's words.

'I love you, Susan. I love Lindy. I'll do my best to make you both happy.'

And the love was there in his eyes, sweet, piercing shafts of love which drew the torment from her soul and implanted a wondrous joy.

'You love me?' she whispered, too choked with emotion to force any more volume.

'With all my heart,' he declared, and the words carried the solemnity of absolute truth.

'No, Susan!' James was forcibly stopping her from going to Dave.

She glared her resentment. 'Let me go! I told you to let me go. I don't want to be with you, James. I love Dave and I'm going to marry him.'

James' face twisted with ugly fury. 'You stupid fool!'

'Let go, Kelleher! You've lost!' Dave commanded in a steely voice.

He clung on for a moment then flung her hands

away. His mouth curled in contempt. 'Go then! Your conventional little mind isn't big enough to appreciate what you could have shared with me.'

The cutting words could not even slice a sliver off Susan's happiness. In an excess of joy and relief she almost threw herself at Dave, hugging him fiercely as he enfolded her in tight security.

'I wish you luck with your ambition, Kelleher,' he tossed at James by way of taking leave.

'No doubt you'll do your best to stab me in the back at every opportunity,' came the acid retort.

'You really shouldn't judge all men by yourself, Kelleher. It's a mistake. Besides, winners can afford to be generous and I happen to like Felicity. Give her my regards.'

With a possessive arm around her waist Dave swept Susan out of the office and along the corridor. Erica Ainsley was spouting terse words at Denise as they entered the reception area. Her cold grey eyes snapped to Susan.

'Miss Hardy, if you . . .'

Dave obviously didn't care for the waspish voice any more than Susan had. 'Save it!' he commanded. 'Whoever you are, madam, you can inform the management that Susan is no longer in their employ.'

'I've just got to get my handbag, Dave,' Susan murmured and darted around the desk, smiling excitedly at an open-mouthed Denise and a temporarily silenced Miss Ainsley. 'Goodbye. Sorry I'm leaving you a bit in the lurch but I'm sure you'll get a replacement for me in no time at all.'

'What is going on?' spluttered Miss Ainsley, losing her cool in a situation which had been completely taken out of her control.

'I'm getting married,' Susan announced gaily and was off with Dave again before the woman could catch her breath.

The lift doors closed. They had the small compartment to themselves and Dave turned her to face him, his eyes searching hers intently. 'Did you mean it when you said you loved me, Susan?'

She curled her arms around his neck, her eyes sparkling assurance until a sudden uncertainty attacked her heart and dimmed all her joy for a moment. 'Didn't you mean it, Dave?'

His mouth curved into a dry little smile. 'Susan, I've been slowly going out of my mind since you dropped Kelleher into my lap on Saturday. That's how you came to get a madman bursting into a law-office to make his last stand, so to speak.'

'It was the best last stand I've ever heard,' she bubbled in happy relief. 'I've been eating my heart out ever since you kissed me and walked away. I thought you didn't want me.'

'Not want you!'

He kissed her with a passion which erased any possible doubt on the matter. Susan responded with all her heart and the love they had hidden from each other exulted in its freedom from all restraint. It surged between them, fed and strengthened by the emotional intensity of its physical expression. They were not aware that the lift had slid to a halt nor that the doors had rolled open. They were totally absorbed in satisfying their needs.

'One way to start off a Monday morning,' a very dry voice commented.

'If you can summon up the energy.'

'You're showing your age, Tommy.'

'Possibly the right stimulus might revive me. I do believe it's our Miss Hardy from reception.'

Susan flushed as she met the amused eyes of Mr O'Toole and Mr McIlroy.

'Excuse us, gentlemen. She's not yours any more. She's mine,' Dave declared blithely, steering Susan out of the compartment and around the two men.

'I say! Aren't you Dave Brown, the cartoonist? You were . . .'

'Correct,' Dave threw over his shoulder. 'And you've just said farewell to the future Mrs Brown.'

Susan laughed up at him, almost delirious with delight at having been granted everything she had wished for. 'I love you, love you, love you, Dave Brown,' she chanted breathlessly.

'I'm just about convinced,' he laughed back at her. 'Let's get out of here.'

He led her across the street where the Riley stood in a no parking zone.

'You could have got fined,' she chided him.

'What's money?' he grinned.

Susan sank into the passenger seat, hugging that beautifully extravagant thought. Dave was so right. It was impossible to put a price on the love they shared. It was unbuyable.

'What made you come for me?' she asked as he took the seat next to her. 'I told you I would finish with James today. Though I must admit your interruption was timely. James wasn't taking kindly to the idea of letting me go.'

Dave expelled a long breath and his eyes held the shadow of pain. 'Susan, I love you so damned much I couldn't bear to take the slightest risk of losing you to Kelleher. Yesterday I thought I'd got you safely drawn my way, but when you said you had to see Kelleher again . . . I spent one hell of a night stewing over that determination of yours. I thought I might have miscalculated . . . that you still wanted him despite the way you had responded to me.'

'No way!' she assured him emphatically. 'I just wanted it definitely finished, that's all. I knew it was you I really loved when you kissed me on Saturday night. Then, when you backed off I thought . . . oh, I felt so dreadfully hollow, Dave.'

'So did I. It took Kelleher to make me realise how much you meant to me and I wanted you like hell.'

In mutual urgency they reached for each other and as mouth claimed mouth their need was an all-consuming fire, a fusion of mind and soul which could never be separated again. Only the physical restraint imposed by the car's bucket seats recalled them to the practical necessity of finding a more suitable place for expressing their love.

'You'd better marry me fast, Susan.'

'Yes. Fast.'

'We'll go to Lamamby this weekend. Get it all arranged with your parents. A proper wedding with all the trimmings. Everyone's to celebrate our marriage. Especially us.'

The marriage ceremony which had been denied to both of them in years gone by. Susan understood his need. It was the echo of her own. Even in this they were together. 'I'd like that, Dave,' she whispered huskily.

The past shimmered briefly between them and was gone. Their eyes glowed with the promise of the future . . . theirs to shape, to have and to hold, from this day forth. And suddenly the urgency of their passion was not so great for they knew there was all the time in the world to savour that final intimacy.

'Let's go to the park,' Susan suggested on a wave of sweet sentiment.

'Want to carve our names on the park bench?' Dave teased.

'We don't have to. It'll always be ours.'

'So it will,' he agreed and they smiled their sure knowledge that the love they shared did not need any print to prove it. 'Somehow I suspect that the grass is going to look greener, the flowers a brighter hue, and the park bench will even feel comfortable.'

Susan laughed and shook her head at him. 'No doubt you're right. You're always right about everything.'

'Not at all. We'll go and see.'

They drove to the park and it was indeed a beautiful place, a comfortable place, a place where they had learnt a sense of belonging which would last them all their lives.

Harlequin Presents

Coming Next Month

911 TO FILL A SILENCE Jayne Bauling
Bustling Taipei sets the scene for a reunion between a free-lance radio reporter and her celebrated ex-husband. He's still as charming and impulsive as ever—the sort of man who'd marry on a whim.

912 TITAN'S WOMAN Ann Chariton
When a powerful Australian developer gives in to a woman's concern for the environment, the newspapers dub them "TITAN and the Amazon." Then he, an experienced infighter, goes straight for the heart!

913 HUNTER'S PREY Jasmine Cresswell
For two years a runaway wife has fled from city to city, state to state, to hide herself and her child from the only man she's ever loved. And now he's found her....

914 WHAT'S RIGHT Melinda Cross
A powerful force draws an interior designer to a wealthy American businessman, though a tragic sense of loyalty binds him to another. But his determination to do what's right only makes her love him more.

915 CHANCE MEETINGS Vanessa James
A man—a rich man—is needed to save her family's Cornish estate. And just like that, two marriageable men happen along—one for Caro and one for her cousin. But nothing's so easy....

916 FIRE WITH FIRE Penny Jordan
When a London newscaster sacrifices everything but her ethics to repay a wily entrepreneur for her sister's recklessness, it occurs to him that he could use a woman like her in his life.

917 A RISKY BUSINESS Sandra K. Rhoades
Risks come with the territory for an Alberta oil scout. But she doesn't plan to risk her heart—not until she's caught snooping around a self-made millionaire's oilfields.

918 LIKE ENEMIES Sophie Weston
With ten-year-old headlines of the family scandal still etched in her mind, a London designer is frightened and confused by her feelings for an alluring international businessman.

Available in September wherever paperback books are sold, or through Harlequin Reader Service:

In the U.S.
P.O. Box 1397
Buffalo, N.Y.
14240-1397

In Canada
P.O. Box 2800, Postal Station A
5170 Yonge Street
Willowdale, Ontario M2N 6J3

A terrible family secret drives Kristi Johannssen to California, where she finds glamor, romance and...a threat to her life!

BEYOND THE RAINBOW

MARGARET CHITTENDEN

Power and elegance, jealousy and deceit, even murder, stoke fires of passion in this glittering novel set in the fashion world of Hollywood, on the dazzling coast of Southern California.

Available in August at your favorite retail outlet, or reserve your copy for July shipping by sending your name, address and zip or postal code along with a check or money order for $4.70 (includes 75¢ for postage and handling) payable to Worldwide Library Reader Service to:

In the U.S.

Worldwide Library
901 Fuhrmann Blvd.
Box 1325
Buffalo, New York
14269-1325

In Canada

Worldwide Library
P.O. Box 2800, 5170 Yonge St.
Postal Station A
Willowdale, Ontario
M2N 6J3

Please specify book title with your order.

((•)) W❂RLDWIDE LIBRARY

BOW-H-1

Take 4 books & a surprise gift FREE

SPECIAL LIMITED-TIME OFFER

Mail to **Harlequin Reader Service®**

In the U.S.
901 Fuhrmann Blvd.
P.O. Box 1394
Buffalo, N.Y. 14240-1394

In Canada
P.O. Box 2800, Station "A"
5170 Yonge Street
Willowdale, Ontario M2N 6J3

YES! Please send me 4 free Harlequin Romance® novels and my free surprise gift. Then send me 6 brand-new novels every month as they come off the presses. Bill me at the low price of $1.65 each ($1.75 in Canada)—a 11% saving off the retail price. There are no shipping, handling or other hidden costs. There is no minimum number of books I must purchase. I can always return a shipment and cancel at any time. Even if I never buy another book from Harlequin, the 4 free novels and the surprise gift are mine to keep forever.

106-BPP-BP6F

Name _____ (PLEASE PRINT)

Address _____ Apt. No. _____

City _____ State/Prov. _____ Zip/Postal Code _____

This offer is limited to one order per household and not valid to present subscribers. Price is subject to change.

DOR-SUB-1R

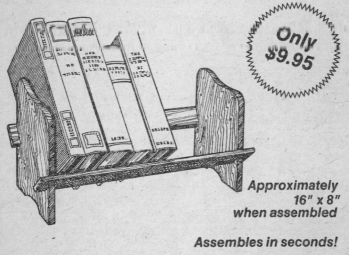

HARLEQUIN HISTORICAL

Explore love with Harlequin in the Middle
Ages, the Renaissance, in the Regency, the
Victorian and other eras.

Relive within these books the endless ages of
romance, set against authentic historical
backgrounds. Two new historical love stories
published each month.

HIST-A-1